Ready, Set, Dough!

Also by Kelly J. Baptist

Isaiah Dunn Saves the Day

Isaiah Dunn Is My Hero

The Swag Is in the Socks

Eb & Flow

Ready, Set, Dough!

KELLY J. BAPTIST

Crown Books for Young Readers
New York

Text copyright © 2023 by Kelly J. Baptist
Jacket art copyright © 2023 by Shannon Wright
Sad face emoji art by Yamonstro used under license from Stock.Adobe.com

All rights reserved. Published in the United States by Crown Books for Young Readers, an imprint of Random House Children's Books, a division of Penguin Random House LLC, New York.

Crown and the colophon are registered trademarks of Penguin Random House LLC.

Visit us on the Web! rhcbooks.com

Educators and librarians, for a variety of teaching tools, visit us at RHTeachersLibrarians.com

Library of Congress Cataloging-in-Publication Data
Names: Baptist, Kelly J., author.
Title: Ready, set, dough! / Kelly J. Baptist.
Description: First edition. | New York: Crown Books for Young Readers, [2023] | Audience: Ages 8–10. | Audience: Grades 4–6. | Summary: Sixth-grader Zoe sets her sights on winning a laptop by becoming the top cookie-dough seller in her class, but as she becomes more obsessed with winning, she begins to lose sight of what is really important.
Identifiers: LCCN 2023010303 (print) | LCCN 2023010304 (ebook) | ISBN 978-0-593-42917-4 (hardcover) | ISBN 978-0-593-42918-1 (library binding) | ISBN 978-0-593-42919-8 (ebook) | ISBN 9780593747711 (ebook)
Subjects: CYAC: Competition—Fiction. | Friendship—Fiction. | Middle schools—Fiction. | Schools—Fiction. | LCGFT: Novels.
Classification: LCC PZ7.1.B3674 Re 2023 (print) | LCC PZ7.1.B3674 (ebook) | DDC [Fic]—dc23

The text of this book is set in 12-point Maxime Pro.
Interior design by Cathy Bobak

Printed in the United States of America
10 9 8 7 6 5 4 3 2 1
First Edition

For every kid out there with big dreams
and goals . . . it's GO time!

Chapter 1

The Art of the Crash

This **CANNOT be happening** right now!

I groan and watch in horror as our ancient computer monitor flickers, fades, and dramatically dies. Okay, let's be real: it's not the first time this computer has betrayed me, but today I'm almost finished typing up my feature article for the school paper! Not a cool time to give up the ghost.

"Mo-om!" I yell downstairs at the exact moment Mom cheerfully calls up, "Zoe! Dinner!"

"Mom, the computer crashed again!" I say, hoping she can tell how serious this is. Maybe she'll drop everything, speed to Office Tech, and buy the Horizon Word-Pro GT, my dream laptop. It's super lightweight, comes in orange (my favorite color), and, according to *WriteOn!* magazine, is "the ultimate machine for serious writers."

Call me obsessed if you want, but I have pictures of the WordPro on my walls and mirror where other people have posters of singers and athletes. It's how I stay motivated. Especially at times like this.

Unfortunately, Mom doesn't see the computer crash as earth-shattering, and she doesn't mention Office Tech or drop what she's doing so we can go. In fact, she does a great job of smiling and carrying the salad bowl and a basket of rolls to the table.

"We'll have someone come look at it," she says breezily. I like that word, *breezily,* just not when it describes my mother's tone when my life is on the line!

"Will you get the ranch dressing?" she asks, like nothing is wrong.

"And Italian," adds my brother, Mark, who's already heaping spaghetti onto his plate. Mark never has to be called for dinner, but you have to scream for him when it's his turn to wash the dishes.

I go to the refrigerator, grab the dressing, and hurry to the table. Maybe if I play the "it's for school" card.

"Mom, my feature article is due tomorrow, and I wasn't finished typing it!"

"Hope you saved it," says Mark, reaching for the dressing. I glare at him and set the bottle down on the opposite end of the table. Mark doesn't even miss a beat. He just stretches his abnormally long arm across the table and grabs it. It takes a lot to get Mark upset.

"Of course I saved it," I tell him, hoping Google has me covered on this one. I scoop up some spaghetti noodles and wait for Mark to finish drowning his plate in Mom's special mushroom-marinara sauce. "But, Mom, we really, *really* need a new computer. You know I do a lot of writing."

"Let's say grace," Mom says, which absolutely frustrates me because it doesn't seem like she gets how important having a computer is. It's hard to pay attention to her prayer because I'm trying to figure out what to say next. Mom beats me to it.

"Zoe, after dinner Mark can take you to the library to finish your report," she says.

"It's an *article*, Mom," I say with a sigh. Why does no one care about my writing?

"Okay, Zoe," Mom says. "You can finish your *article* at the library."

"I have practice tonight, Mom," Mark says, his mouth full of Mom's homemade roll. And, of course, his stupid band will probably take priority over what *I* need to do.

"Hmm." Mom thinks for a moment as she nibbles on her salad. "Are you all practicing at Chad's?"

"Mm-hmm." Mark nods.

"Do they have a computer and printer?" Mom asks.

"Yeah, probably." Mark shrugs. He's obviously not getting it, but I see exactly where this is going.

"Well, can your sister go with you and use their computer while you guys practice?"

"Mom, no!" I say. I can't believe she'd rather have me around four rowdy teenage boys than safe in my own room with a Horizon WordPro GT!

Surprisingly, Mark doesn't protest the way I do, because as long as he gets to play his music, he doesn't really care what else is happening around him.

"I'll text Chad," he says, before heaping more food onto his plate.

"Mom, can't Daddy just take me to the library?"

And then to Office Tech. . . .

"He's working late tonight," Mom says, and her face changes a tiny bit before going back to normal. It's like when a cloud moves in front of the sun for a second, so I call it her Shadow Face. She's been getting it more and more lately.

"So why don't you just go with Mark tonight, Zoe," Mom continues, her Shadow Face gone, "and I'll work on getting the computer fixed for next time."

I sigh loudly, but I know my fate has been sealed and there's no use protesting anymore. I'll work on Daddy in the morning. He's usually bright and sunny once he gets his cup of coffee. And hey, he recently bought this expensive coffee machine because he loves coffee, so he of all people should understand how much I need the WordPro because I love writing. Plus, the WordPro isn't *that* expensive, so it should be easy to convince him.

"Let's go, Zo," Mark says, his plate completely clean. His guitar and amp are already placed neatly by the door, so all he has to do is throw on his coat. I, on the other hand, have half a plate of spaghetti left, and unlike Mark, I actually like to taste my food while I'm eating it.

"Can I at least finish my food?" I ask, chewing slowly.

"Mom, if she's going with me, we gotta leave now. Chad's parents only let us play till eight," Mark says.

"I don't blame them," Mom says under her breath. No one really knows how Chad's parents survive the noise of the so-called band.

"Zoe, just take your plate with you," she says, which is a total shock.

"I thought we weren't allowed to eat in the car," I reply.

"I'll make an exception since your brother's doing me a favor. Get your coat so you don't make him late."

Are you kidding me? No one shows any real concern for a *school*-related article I need to write, but I have to break rules and risk indigestion and possible hearing loss for Mark's stupid band rehearsal? Not fair!

I sigh loudly again, but this time Mom gives me *the look,* so I cut it short. I call it her Buttons Face, as in, *Keep*

5

pushing my buttons and see what happens. You don't mess with the Buttons Face.

"Bye, Mom," I say as I drag myself to the garage, where Mark already has the car on and his music cranked up loud.

"Bye, sweetie," she says with a smile. "And no worries; we'll have the computer up and running in no time."

But that's exactly what I'm worried about. Because if they do fix the Crash Machine, the only WordPro I'll have is the one that's taped on my wall.

Chapter 2

Saved by the CRIM

So much for a cozy evening of writing. I barely have my document opened on the Whitfields' computer when the noise starts up. Even though I'm way upstairs in the loft area, and the band is way downstairs in the basement, I can hear Beanie's loud mouth as if he were right here screaming in my ear. I think they should be a band that just plays instruments, but sometimes Beanie gets the urge to "sing," as he calls it.

Beanie's the bass player of the band, Mark plays lead guitar, Rodney's on the keyboard, and Chad plays the drums. Beanie's real name is Ivan, so they decided to name the band the CRIM, which is all their initials put together. Daddy jokes that they better not get an Elliot or Ethan to join the band, cuz then they'd be the CRIME. Personally, I think the name fits; their music *is* a crime.

"Ugh!" I groan loudly, but no one is there to hear it. Chad's parents are up in their room with earplugs in, most likely reading. They're both college professors who are probably wondering how they got stuck with a wild child like Chad.

I munch on one of the oatmeal chocolate chip cookies that Chad's mother gave me and try to tune out the CRIM. Most people don't realize how hard it is to write a good article. Not hard like geometry or Spanish, of course. More like the hard in doing one of Mom's video workouts. You really gotta push yourself, but then you feel good when it's done. At least, that's what Mom says.

I work on the Who's Buzzin' column, which features a new student or teacher every week. When there's a special event or issue going on, we also do a What's Buzzin' column. This week, I'm doing a feature on Mr. Stinson, the seventh-grade social studies teacher. Rumor is, he's gonna be retiring soon, but when I hinted at it (trying to get the scoop), he just flashed his yellow teeth; coughed for, like, a minute straight; and said he had plenty of good years left. I made sure to get that quote.

Mr. Stinson is obviously really old, but he's also extremely boring, which is making this article pretty hard to write. Most times, my subject has a cool hobby or a juicy little-known fact to share, but Mr. Stinson gave me none of that in our interview. He rattled on about his love of history, which I thought was so cliché for a guy who's basically a living history book. He's nothing like Mrs. Lyles, the art teacher. She's probably as old as Mr. Stinson but way cooler. She travels every summer to places like Paris and Venice and Athens and Cape Town, and has a wall of postcards in her classroom.

Usually only seventh and eighth graders get to be on the *Kentwood Buzz,* our school's paper, but this year they decided to pick three sixth graders to be junior staff members and take a journalism elective class. I'm one of the sixth graders, and so is my best friend, Felix Fields, who's a junior photographer. It won't be *junior* for long, though; Felix works miracles with his camera! Some of the other kids didn't think sixth graders would be able to do a good job, but me and Felix are proving them all wrong.

Until now.

If I can't get this article together, they might kick me off the staff. I brainstorm all the words that come to me when I think of Mr. Stinson, but none of them are cool or eye-catching enough for a headline.

And then the unthinkable happens.

Before I can stop myself, I accidentally start listening to the words that Beanie is screeching:

"REWIND! REWIND! Free yourself from now, go back in time!"

And I actually get an idea! Writing a typical question-and-answer article on Mr. Stinson would bore everybody to death, but maybe there's something from our interview that I can turn into more of a fictional piece. Thanks to the CRIM, I now have my headline: "Rewinding Herbert Stinson."

"Hmm, there's gotta be something here," I mumble as I go through my notes. I have to fight the yawns even as I read his answers to my questions. I mean, who studies Greek for fun and only listens to cassette tapes? What are cassette tapes anyway? I do a quick search and nearly die laughing. People used to buy these bulky rectangle-block things to listen to music? I make a face and wonder if my parents did.

As I keep reading, it hits me: the cassette tape thing totally goes with my headline! I start typing, and before too long I have an awesome story about a much younger Mr. Stinson getting his very first cassette tape, and how amazing and new it was at that time. I don't like bragging, but it's a pretty good piece, especially considering what I had to work with. I upload the file to the *Buzz*'s shared drive and share it with myself and Felix, just to be safe.

I pop another cookie into my mouth and grab my phone to text Felix.

> Felix, no lie, I just wrote my BEST STORY EVER!

> And it's about Mr. Stinson! Make sure you bring your camera tomorrow! It'll be hard, but we can try to get at least one good pic of him.

Felix usually responds super-fast, just always with short responses. This time it takes him two whole minutes, which I don't have the patience for. And, of course, he always adds his annoying, unfunny hashtag to the message:

> Cool. And duh, all my pics are GOOD #upgrade

I growl at my phone, which is embarrassingly old since it used to be Mark's, like, eighty years ago. My parents actually wrapped it up and gave it to me as a "gift" for my birthday last year. Daddy said it was my trial phone, to see how I do with it before they spend actual money on one. Get this: they didn't even put me on the family plan! That means I, Zoe Sparks, journalism genius, can only use my phone when I'm around Wi-Fi! What a slap in the face! Felix never lets me forget it.

> Don't start, Fe Fe. Are you covering the assembly?

> Yup.

Felix and I always have fun at assemblies. We have the tradition of whispering what we think the teachers up front are thinking. The funniest thing ever was when the entire PA system crashed and burned just when Felix whispered that Ms. Mason *had* to be thinking about how annoying her voice was.

Mrs. Whitfield's soft touch on my shoulder almost makes me jump out of my skin. Since I have on headphones and the CRIM is so loud, the whole house could've been robbed and I wouldn't know.

"How're you doing, Zoe?"

"Oh, um, I'm okay, Mrs. Whitfield," I say, pulling off the headphones.

"Sorry, I didn't mean to startle you," Mrs. Whitfield says, yelling to be heard over the band. "Just making sure you're surviving this!"

Mrs. Whitfield smiles, but I can tell she's had enough of the noise.

"Greg and I can't take much more," she tells me, checking her watch. The time on the computer says 7:35. The torture is almost over!

"Do you mind if I print this?" I ask. Even though the article is uploaded and saved, I always like to keep hard copies of my articles. I've had one too many computer disasters where I've ended up losing something important.

"Sure!" Mrs. Whitfield shows me which printer to connect to (they have two; no fair!), and before I know it, my words float into the world on crisp white paper.

I scan the Whitfields' office setup: computer, laptop, one of those printers that also scans and faxes, electric stapler, wireless keyboard, a box of printer paper, ink cartridges for days, a paper shredder. Even the wireless mouse is cool! They have the ideal everything in this loft, and I bet Chad never even sets foot up here. I sigh. He doesn't know how lucky he is. All he cares about is his drums. But hey, if I had a setup like this in my room, you'd probably never see me, either.

At 7:55, I start shutting everything down. I eject my thumb drive and put it in the inside pouch of my backpack. The article goes in an orange folder that's supposedly waterproof, but I won't be the one testing that theory. At exactly 8:00, a wave of silence covers the house. YESSSS! The Whitfields have Chad trained well; one of them always flickers the lights in the basement at 7:59, and if the music doesn't stop at 8:00 on the dot, Chad is on a drum restriction for a week. The CRIM learned quickly that Mr. and Mrs. Whitfield mean business.

I sling my bag over my shoulder and trudge down the stairs to the kitchen after one last goodbye to the Whitfield writing paradise. The guys are all bringing their instruments upstairs, laughing, loud, and stinky.

"Bro, that last fill was monster," Beanie tells Chad.

"Imagine Mr. Gerrard's face if you did that in class!" Rodney adds. They all laugh.

"Ahhh, nice, my mom made cookies!" Chad says, noticing the plate on the island. I feel like I'm watching Animal Planet as they devour the cookies like a pack of lions. Chad pours giant glasses of milk for them and finishes off the gallon himself. Massive burps follow. Gross.

"W'sup, Zo Zo?" Beanie says, and it's like they all notice me for the first time.

"Hey," I tell him.

"When you gonna sing lead for us?" Rodney jokes.

"Ummm, from how Beanie sounded?" I say, making a face. "Soon."

"Ooooh!"

The guys bust up laughing and throw playful punches at Beanie, who crosses his arms in protest.

"Why you gotta come for me, Zoe?" he complains. "Mark, man, get your sister."

Beanie's lucky. I could say a *lot* more about all of them. They're like having extra Marks, though, which means their revenge tactics are intense, and I'm way outnumbered.

"You finish your stuff?" Mark asks.

"Yes." I turn and smile sweetly at Chad. "Thank you, Chadwick, for the use of your computer equipment."

Only his parents call him Chadwick, and I know he hates it. He throws a piece of cookie at me, which is dumb. He has two older sisters, but they're both away at college, so I know it'll be him who has to clean the crumbs up.

"Yo, tell your parents to step into this century and get a Mac or something," Chad tells Mark. One thing we agree on.

The guys launch into some music conversation, using terms that make no sense to me. I clear my throat. Mark glares at me.

"Chill, Zoe," he says. He rolls his eyes and tells the guys, "It's her bedtime."

Ugh! I hate when he does that. I'm six years younger than him but probably way more mature. And it is *not* my bedtime; I just wanna get home and talk to Daddy about getting a computer. If he's home yet, that is.

Mark finally says goodbye to the rest of the CRIM, and we climb into Mom's old Subaru, which is cold and covered with a dusting of snow. We both blow on our hands while we wait for the car to heat up. Mark blasts music the whole way home. It's some playlist Beanie made, and it almost sounds as bad as their band does.

I don't see Daddy's Jeep when Mark presses the button to open the garage. Oh well. I'll have a few extra hours to strategize for the morning.

"How'd it go?" Mom asks. She's curled up on the couch, flipping through a magazine when we come inside.

"Apart from the fact that I lost hearing in both my ears—"

Mark swats my shoulder on his way upstairs.

"Whatever," he says. "It was a great practice, Mom!"

Mom sighs.

"I meant your assignment," she says to me.

"Yes, I got my article done," I tell her. I sit down and make my face sweet and innocent. "It would've been much easier if—"

"Zoe." Mom cuts me off with a warning tone. "Don't start."

"Okay, okay," I grumble. Guess I'll have to save all my ammunition for Daddy. When I win a Pulitzer Prize, I'll be sure to include this moment in my speech. I'll tell the world that I produce masterpieces despite being denied proper equipment as a young, impressionable girl.

"Go get ready for bed, Zoe," Mom says, interrupting my daydream. She yawns herself, but I don't dare say what I'm thinking—that maybe she's the one who should be going to bed.

"'Kay," I say, standing up so she knows I'm on my way to doing what she said. I have one more question, though.

"Is Daddy coming home soon, or does he have to close?"

Mom's Shadow Face flashes for a second, and I wish Felix were here to take a picture of it. I could write a whole feature on that face.

"He's closing tonight," Mom says.

"Oh. Well, good night."

"Good night."

I glance over my shoulder at Mom as I go up the stairs. She's not looking at the magazine anymore but staring off at I don't know what. Maybe it's a good thing Daddy's not home yet. It doesn't seem like the best time to mention the WordPro. As I'm brushing my teeth, I remember one of Daddy's favorite sayings. *It's always better in the morning.*

I hope so.

Chapter 3

Coffee Isn't Magic

"Heeey, Daddy-o!" I say as cheerfully as I can after waking up with my ears still ringing from last night with the CRIM. Daddy's leaning against the counter, scrolling on his non-ancient phone and sipping what I'm hoping is his second cup of coffee.

"Hey, Zo Zo," Daddy says, not even looking up. "Cereal today."

Translation: neither he nor Mom felt like cooking breakfast. Most mornings, one of them will make pancakes or oatmeal or light, fluffy biscuits. I guess this is not one of those mornings.

"No worries; I can dig it!" I keep the cheery attitude going and check Daddy's face. A tiny smile. He stays glued to his phone, though. O-kaaaay, time for Phase II.

"TGIF, right?"

I cringe right after I say it. Daddy's a manager at Palace Farms, a grocery store chain in our area. Most weeks, Fridays are nothing to get excited about for him. He probably has to work tomorrow.

Daddy grunts and keeps swiping. He's wearing his typical outfit: khakis and a green Palace Farms polo. When I was little, he'd always say, "Well, I'm off to the Palace!" whenever he went to work. I thought it was so cool. Back then the store used to pass out gold crowns to kids in the checkout lanes, kinda like how banks give lollipops. I used to collect those crowns and play with them like they were dolls. Embarrassing. Anyway, they don't even have those crowns anymore, and now Daddy just says, "I'm going to work."

"It wasn't a bad rehearsal last night," I say casually, reaching for the Honey Bunches of Oats.

"Mmmm, that's good."

"You know I had to go with Mark because of the computer crash," I add, in case he doesn't know. Daddy sighs and looks up.

"Zoe—"

He thinks I'm about to fuss about the computer. Not exactly.

"Mark's getting pretty good on guitar," I say, cutting Daddy off.

"Is he." Daddy says this like a statement, not a question.

The phone is on the counter now, and he's watching me like he knows I'm up to something.

"Yup." I pour milk over my cereal and grab a spoon. "I think the practice is helping him."

I crunch on my cereal for a while, pretend to read everything on the box. It's a good thing Mark starts school before me, otherwise he'd see right through all this "Mark plays really good" stuff. Daddy picks up his phone again.

"How long has he been playing?" I ask.

"Probably six, seven years," Daddy says.

"So that means he started when he was about my age," I say. "That's a good age to start something, right?"

"What's up, Zoe?" Daddy says. "What are you getting at?"

"I'm just saying, Mark got his first guitar six or seven years ago, and he's getting really good now. That means your investment paid off, right?"

Daddy chuckles and sits down at the table across from me.

"You're not slick, Zoe," he says, shaking his head. At least there's a piece of a smile on his face.

"Huh?" I give him my sweet and innocent face and he laughs.

" 'Huh?' " He imitates me. " 'Mark's sounding really good these days!' "

"I do NOT sound like that," I tell him. "And he is!"

"Uh-huh," Daddy says. "What do you want, Zoe?"

"I don't want anything, Daddy," I say. "But what I really, really, *really* need is the Horizon WordPro GT! It'll be just like when you guys got Mark a guitar cuz he wanted to play. Only better! Your investment will pay off way more with me. Imagine being in the audience while your only daughter accepts a prestigious writing award and thanks her wonderful parents for buying her very first laptop! That could be you!"

"You are something else," Daddy says. He says that a lot about me. I'm not sure what *something else* is, but I'm hoping it's good.

"So is the WordPro!" I say. "It's the best writing machine on the market, especially for a young, budding talent like me."

"And I bet it has the 'best' price tag on it as well," Daddy says. "How much?"

"How much was Mark's guitar?" I counter.

"First of all," Daddy says, giving me a look—yikes, I better watch it!—"that's none of your concern. And second of all, when your grandfather died, Grandma decided to give his guitar to your brother. You think Grandpop had an old laptop in the attic that you can have?"

Now it's Daddy's turn to ask a snarky question. I sigh. But, of course, I don't give up that easily. I just have to choose what I say carefully. My whole argument is messed up by the fact that they never bought Mark's first guitar. I can't argue that he has a new one *now*, because a few summers ago, Mark worked as a cart boy at Palace Farms to buy it. I'm too young to get an official job like that, and since Grandpop didn't leave me a laptop, it's not fair to make me wait till I'm old enough.

I stop eating my cereal and see Daddy studying me. He chuckles.

"I can see the wheels spinning in your head, Zo Zo," he says. "You might've missed your calling; you'd make a great lawyer."

I fight the urge to roll my eyes, cuz Daddy doesn't play that type of thing. But it's *beyond* frustrating that he doesn't get it. I know exactly what I want to be: a journalist. Not a lawyer, not a florist, not a grocery store manager, and definitely not a terrible musician.

I put my spoon down. Not even hungry anymore. I also can't bring myself to begin Phase III, the last resort, which is to ask if they can at least fix our current excuse-for-a-computer. I'm forever doomed to have to write at the library or the Whitfields' home office, not free to roam with the very portable WordPro, in its specially manufactured carrying case.

"Calm down, Zoe," Daddy says, checking his watch. "You're being dramatic."

Other words I hear ALL the time. *Calm down, Zoe! Stop being dramatic, Zoe.*

"It's *passion*, Daddy," I say, like I always do.

"Right," Daddy says, getting up from the table. "Why don't you *passionately* finish that cereal and grab your coat so we can go."

Man, when your dad works around food all day, you can never waste it. In my humble but intelligent opinion, he shouldn't even care, cuz he can always just grab a gallon of milk and another box before he comes home.

I eat the rest of my soggy flakes and grab my backpack and coat. It's always awkward to lose a battle with a parent and then have to ride with them to school, but Daddy acts like we didn't just have a moment in the kitchen. Probably because the conversation meant absolutely nothing to him. He's happily whistling some song from the nineties.

Until he turns the key to the Jeep.

Nothing.

He tries it again, but the Jeep won't start. Daddy stops whistling.

"Really?" he asks no one in particular. He sighs and pops the hood. After a few minutes of looking around under there, he's on the phone with Cedric, our mechanic, and then Mom.

Mom normally works afternoons at a floral shop downtown, but her hours always pick up around holidays. With Valentine's Day right around the corner, she's been going in earlier than usual and sometimes staying late.

"He can't get here till one at the earliest," Daddy says

into his cell when he climbs into the car. "Just what we need, right?"

I can hear Mom's voice but not what she's saying. Hopefully it's something like, "Calm down, honey; you're being dramatic."

"Mom's gonna come and pick us up," he tells me once they hang up. My watch says 8:20. Mom's job is about fifteen minutes away, and my school is about ten minutes away. The calculations add up to me being late. Again. The last time, Daddy had some emergency inventory meeting at the store that he remembered at the last minute, so he couldn't take me to school. By the time Mom got herself ready to go, womp womp. Late.

I tap my foot on the floor, like that will make Mom speed up or time slow down. Daddy drums his fingers on the steering wheel, like that will make Cedric magically appear. Since we're stuck in the car with nothing else to do, I decide to try again.

"So, Daddy, about the WordPro. . . . What if I help pay for it?"

"Zoe, doesn't your school give you Chromebooks?"

"Huh?"

"Chromebooks," Daddy says. "I remember them going on and on about them at the back-to-school bash."

"Well, yeah," I say, "but we can't bring them home, thanks to Jordan Washington and his stupid friends."

I tell Daddy how this group of eighth graders tried to sell their Chromebooks on eBay last year. After that disaster, we weren't allowed to take them home anymore. What I hate the most is that they ruined it for the rest of us but don't even have to deal with the consequences because they're in high school now.

"Well, it's something," Daddy says. There should be a limit on how many times a parent can completely miss the point.

When Mom pulls into the driveway, it's 8:39 and counting, which means the late bell already rang, and everyone is probably in the gym for the assembly. Daddy and I scramble into her car, and at least it's warm.

"Hey, Zoe," she calls over her shoulder to me.

"Hey."

Mom and Daddy talk about what might be wrong with the Jeep and how much it might cost. I squeeze my lips together so I don't accidentally say how dramatic they sound. We hit every red light in town and get to my school at 8:52. It makes absolutely no sense to run.

"Can one of you come in to excuse my tardy?" I ask.

"I gotta get your dad to work, Zoe," Mom says, pointing at the clock on her dashboard. Of course, it's okay for *me* to be late, but not him. "Tell them I'll call and excuse it."

I close the car door without saying goodbye, and Mom peels off without waiting to make sure I actually get inside the building. I know she'll get busy with stuff and forget to call the attendance office.

When I walk inside the office, Ms. Hamilton, the secretary, is sipping coffee from a pink thermos. I don't know what it is with adults and coffee, but it doesn't seem to make their moods any better.

"Good morning, Ms. Hamilton!" I say, turning on the cheeriness like I'm not almost thirty minutes late. "TGIF, right?"

She doesn't even smile. She sips and grunts.

"I believe this is your third unexcused tardy, Ms. Sparks," she says, already writing my slip. "You know that's an automatic detention. You can serve it on Monday."

"Thank you, Ms. Hamilton," I say when she hands me both slips. I'm careful not to sound *too* sarcastic. Ms. Hamilton has been known to snap at kids for no reason, and Principal Bledsoe always believes whatever she says.

As I trudge down the empty hallway, I imagine buying the WordPro myself and writing something amazing. Maybe I'll write about how to overcome the obstacles adults throw your way. Maybe I'll just write about how to turn a crappy Friday around.

First, I'll have to figure out if that's even possible.

Chapter 4

Turning a Crappy Friday Around

Kentwood Academy is set up like a honeycomb hive, which I guess makes sense because our mascot is a hornet. But wait, do hornets even live in hives, or do they have nests? I should maybe say something about this to Principal Bledsoe.

Anyway, our building is the only K-8 in the area and it's divided into pods, three upstairs and three downstairs. The sixth-grade pod is upstairs, and as I'm going up, I can hear the "Baby Shark" song drifting over from the kindergarten/first-grade pod. Mark says the song seems cute but it's really programming little kids to take over the world. Judging from the screams coming from their area, he might be right.

I have Mr. Boyd for homeroom this year, and Felix does, too. We've been in the same classroom since third grade, so I guess the scheduling people aren't paying close attention. Me and Felix make a bet at the end of every school year, and he always bets we'll be together. So for the past three years, I've had to buy him a box of ice cream sandwiches, which he eats all at once cuz they're banned at his house.

"Welcome, Zoe," Mr. Boyd says mid-sentence. His voice is kinda monotone, but that's normal for him. His name is Robert, but kids call him *Robot* Boyd or Mr. Bored because of how he talks. He's probably my parents' age, but he dresses like Mr. Stinson, wearing corduroy pants and sweater-vests all the time. Other than that, he's an okay teacher, even if mornings with him take *forever*!

After I hand Mr. Boyd my tardy slip and walk to my seat, I catch Felix's eye. He's making the *Yikes!* face. Felix keeps track of my tardies just as much as Ms. Hamilton. I shrug. Not my fault.

In my opinion, having to start the day with math is a tragedy. I tried telling Principal Bledsoe this during orientation in August, but we didn't see eye to eye. She's one tough lady. That's okay, though; we have two and a half more years together. It *has* to get better.

While Mr. Boyd talks about improper fractions, I jot down story ideas. The cafeteria food story is so cliché, but they just served something last week that was *supposed* to be chili. Epic fail. Rumor is, a few kids in the lower school got food poisoning, so maybe we could get away with doing a story on this. I write down, *"We shouldn't be afraid of lunch"* and *"A menu of truth"* for headlines. Not sure about that first one. Miss Douglas, our journalism teacher, said my story ideas are unique and bold but maybe too provocative for sixth grade. I looked up *provocative*, by the way. It means tending to provoke, excite, or deliberately cause a strong reaction. Doesn't sound bad to me at all. In fact, that's what news stories should do, right? I guess Miss Douglas should know; she's the real deal. She works for WKLV Channel 54 News, and let me tell you, she is #goals. Not that I would want to work for a news station in the morning and then come teach a journalism class in the afternoons, but hey, she says she's blessed to be able to do both her passions every day.

Anyway, though it's true that we shouldn't be afraid our lunch will make us sick, Miss Douglas would probably call my headline too provocative. Maybe I can come at the story a different way. We could feature one of the lunch ladies in the next Who's Buzzin' column. I'd start off nice and easy, learn about their life and kids and stuff, then BAM! I'd uncover what they're *really* putting in the food.

"Zoe? Why don't you take a swing at this one?"

Huh?

I blink and see Mr. Boyd looking at me, an excited grin on his face. He literally swings his arms like he's holding

29

a bat. I stare at the whiteboard. Okay, twenty-eight over nine; we're changing improper fractions to mixed numbers. I think that means I have to divide?

See, that's why I hate math! Words are so much easier. They mean what they mean and you don't have to divide them all over the place.

"Give it a try," Mr. Boyd says. "You can check your notes. Looks like you were taking good ones."

Wait. A. Second. Is Mr. Boyd challenging me on the low? I absolutely hate when teachers do that! But he still has that *You can do it!* grin on his face, so I decide he's probably just being himself.

Out of the corner of my eye, I see Felix shaking his head. He sits a row behind me and to the left, so I can't get an easy hint from him.

"Ummm, we have to divide, right?" I ask.

"Duh!" someone behind me whispers. I fight the urge to whirl around to see who it is.

"Correct," Mr. Boyd says. "And if you have a remaining amount, it becomes your numerator."

I want to tell Mr. Boyd that his explanation only confused me more, but instead I turn on the brain power and blurt, "Three and one over nine," after a few seconds.

"You got it!" Mr. Boyd says, giving me a thumbs-up and moving on to someone else. I peek over at Felix, and he's got a huge smirk on his face. He probably knew the answer to the problem before Mr. Boyd even finished writing it. I stick my tongue out at him.

After math, earth science, and computer technology with Mr. Boyd, we have lunch, then head to Ms. Price for social studies and language arts. Electives are last hour, and that's when Felix and I have journalism, aka the best class in the world.

"Whatcha doing this weekend?" I ask Felix while Ms. Price sets up a video for us. I already know what he's gonna say.

"Hanging at the restaurant, swim training, the usual," Felix says. "You?"

"Well, it won't be writing, that's for sure," I tell him, still grumpy about our computer situation. "Unless I escape to the library. Ugh! How messed up is that?"

"Library's cool," Felix says with a shrug.

Sometimes I don't know how we're friends. I'm like white water rafting, and he's like . . . inner tubes on the lazy river. I could tell him I got hit by a car, have amnesia, or am moving to Thailand, and he'd be like, "At least you're still alive," "Now everything's new for you," or "We can always use Zoom." See how annoying that is? He doesn't even understand what a dilemma I'm in.

"Whatever, Fe Fe," I say. He stares death daggers at

me because I'm using the nickname he absolutely abhors. I made it up in first grade when he was the only one who listened to my news stories at recess. I probably still have some old copies of my Zo Zo and Fe Fe columns under my bed somewhere.

"Chill with that," Felix tells me. I just laugh. I guess they're right about opposites attracting.

Ms. Price passes worksheets around and starts the video. Dang, that means we really gotta pay attention; she sometimes phrases her questions in ways that you won't get if you're doing other things instead of listening and watching. I miss a few fill-in-the-blank questions because another article idea hits me about halfway through the video.

"Hey, Felix, what'd you get for seventeen?" I whisper.

"Shhhh!" he whispers back. I suck my teeth. He should know better than to think I'm gonna give up this easy.

"What about eighteen?" I whisper.

"Pay attention!" he hisses.

"I am!"

It's just . . . when an idea comes, I have no choice but to explore it right away. It's not my fault Felix doesn't take his photography as seriously as I do writing.

My personal opinion? Felix does too much. He's good in school (probably because he has to be; his parents don't play!), is an awesome photographer, swims in the winter, runs track and field in the spring, and can already make roti like nobody's business. Mom's always saying he's soooo well-rounded, but meh. Why be good at a million different things when you can be life-changingly AH-MAZING at one? He makes it real hard on the rest of us. But still. . . .

I nudge Mr. Perfect with my foot.

"Nineteen?"

"Aztecs, Incas, and Mayans. Now leave me alone!"

"Thanks!" I say, and scramble to put those in the right order while listening to the narrator for the next answer. Once I'm caught up, I force my brain to hold all creative thoughts until last hour. Language arts is kinda cool, cuz we're decoding poems, but I don't really have that "Ahhhh!" feeling until the bell rings and we walk over to the eighth-grade pod for journalism.

Including Felix, there are only four boys in journalism, and I'm pretty sure they're either here because they waited too long to choose an elective or because they like Miss Douglas.

"Hey, guys, TGIF!" Miss Douglas says as we file in and take our seats. I gotta admit, she doesn't *at all* look like she's been up since 3:30 a.m. Other teachers, who shall remain nameless, walk around like they woke up ten minutes before they had to be at work. Hey, maybe that's a decent idea that's not too provocative: school start times.

I'm sure both kids and teachers would agree that school starts too early and lasts too long. I open my idea notebook and write, *"ABC's or zzzzz's: Why not have both?"* I can feel it; this is golden!

"Yo, Miss Douglas, you got my article?" asks Amari. He's definitely here because of Miss Douglas.

"Yes, I did, Amari, and your story had a nice splash of humor." Miss Douglas flashes him a smile before turning to the rest of us. "I was able to review all articles for next week's newsletter. Good work, everyone. Zoe, loved what you did with your piece on Mr. Stinson. Looking for more of that magic this month."

I think about being low-key about Miss Douglas's comment, but I grin till my cheeks hurt. We all take in the kudos; it's not always like this. Sometimes our articles are trash, and Miss Douglas goes in on us. As cool as she is, she's also demanding. She's always saying, "Excellence should be your number one goal."

Fridays in journalism class are usually pretty chill. We work on getting our newsletter right and tight and ready for Monday. We also get started on articles for the following week. But before we do all that, Miss Douglas passes some papers to us.

"Fundraiser time!" she says. "Kentwood's spring fundraiser officially kicks off today and will run for three weeks. Proceeds will benefit field trips and clubs, including our amazing Journalism Club, which meets on Wednesdays after school, by the way."

A few kids groan when they see the fundraiser packet. Brandon Myers, an eighth grader who's a tad bit scary, balls his up and throws it away before Miss Douglas is even done talking.

" 'Dough for Dough'? Really?" Felix reads the theme of the fundraiser and laughs. "Corny!"

I barely hear anything anyone says, though, because my eyes are glued to the list of prizes. Sell five items, get a yo-yo; sell twenty, get a glow-in-the-dark T-shirt. Blah blah blah. But when I get to the top—the cream-of-the-crop prizes—my heart stops.

Yeah, there's this cool drone thingy. But there's also a Horizon WordPro GT.

THERE'S A HORIZON WORDPRO GT!!

I punch Felix on the shoulder, harder than I should, actually, because he yelps. I'm so excited I can't even speak at first. I just point at the prize list. And point. And point.

"What, Zoe?" Felix rubs his shoulder and glares at me. "Dang!"

"Felix, look!" I sound like a three-year-old in the American Girl doll store, but I don't even care.

"A drone? So?"

I could smack him!

"It's *the* laptop! *My* laptop!"

Felix peers at the sheet again.

"Oh."

Oh? OH?? Man, it must be nice to have parents who buy you a fancy camera just cuz you decide you want to take pictures. Or put you in swim camps because you like swimming. All I want is one little laptop, and my parents won't even get that! The one thing they know I want! I stare at the page some more. Zoe Mode kicks in.

"I'm gonna get it."

"Okaaay," Felix says, leaning over to study the page more closely. "School's top seller gets their choice of grand prizes. Asterisk, must sell at least fifty items."

Yes, Felix literally said the word *asterisk*.

"You saw that part, Zo?" he asks. Super-annoying.

"Yeah," I say. "So?"

"So you're gonna sell fifty tubs of cookie dough in three weeks?"

"Yes, Felix, if it means I get the WordPro."

Felix shrugs, and I already know what he's gonna say next.

"I'll help you if you want."

"She'll need all the help she can get!"

Felix and I both whirl around to see the smirking face of Amaya Shaw. She's the third sixth grader who writes for the newsletter, and me and her have been at odds since kindergarten. Who even knows why?

"Really, Zoe? Fifty tubs?" Amaya has a big *Yeah, right* all over her face.

"Well, how nice of you to be in my business," I say, rolling my eyes.

"You were talking loud enough," Amaya says. She makes her voice all high and squeaky. "It's the Horizon WordPro GT! It's the Horizon WordPro GT!"

I glare at her.

"Zoe." Felix puts a hand on my desk. He already knows what's coming, but it's not something he can stop.

"What's your problem, Amaya?" I growl.

"Oh, no problem at all," Amaya says, putting on this innocent front. "It's just, you're so excited about that cheap laptop, I hope you'll be okay with *not* getting it. I mean, I can get fifty sales in *one week* at my dad's job."

"Amaya, chill with all that," Felix says.

"I'm just sayin'," she says, all singsongy.

Amaya's always bragging about how her dad buys her anything she wants because he makes soooo much money. We all know he works at one of those fancy buildings downtown, but she's never said exactly what he does. Mom says people like Amaya are really insecure; that's why they have to brag about what they have or what they do. I don't know about that, though. Amaya seems overly confident to me—way worse than Felix—and what she says next makes me see red.

"I've never been top seller before," she says, finally walking to her own seat. She shrugs. "Guess there's a first time for everything."

Miss Douglas is talking about how the homeroom with the most sales will win a trip to Pizza Zone. Some kids get hyped about this, but not me. Mark works there part-time, saving for a new guitar amp. There's pizza, there are games, blah blah blah. Pizza Zone definitely isn't my goal, but it'll be a benefit on the way. I'm gonna sell so much cookie dough that not only will I get the WordPro, our homeroom with Mr. Boyd will get that party, too.

Chapter 5

Goin' to Church

Felix is an idea genius! Been that way since I met him. Of course, I'll never tell him in those exact words, but I can't help thinking it now, with him and his family on the way to pick me up.

"Bye, Mom!" I call when I hear the car horn in the driveway.

"Bye, Zoe!" Mom calls from her bedroom. She's usually awake by now, but I guess the extra hours at her job are starting to get to her. Daddy's already at work, and Mark up at nine-thirty on a Saturday morning? Forget about it.

I check myself in the mirror before throwing on my coat. Felix said I could wear whatever, so I have on a tan sweater dress with orange leggings and my snuggly warm faux-fur boots. I ate a bagel and an apple for breakfast, so I do a quick teeth check. My hair's more poofy than curly today, but it'll have to do. It's my trademark style anyway. I'm out the door before Mrs. Fields, Felix's mom, can beep again.

I usually ride with the Fieldses after school during the week, so I'm used to their kinda-cluttered minivan. Mr. and Mrs. Fields own Mango Bay, a Caribbean restaurant that's right down the street from Snowflower, the floral shop where Mom works. I hang at either place until Mom is ready to go home. Yesterday, it was Mango Bay. Felix and I took over a booth in the corner and strategized about how I'm gonna be Kentwood's top seller. Felix's first idea was that I go to church with them today. He said it's youth day and that they're having food after the service.

"You can set up a table in the basement and sell cookie dough then," Felix had said. "Everybody will be in this 'Support our kids!' mood, so it might be good."

See what I mean? Genius.

"Good maaaahning!" Mrs. Fields sings as I climb into the bucket seat beside Felix.

"Good morning," I say. Can't help but smile whenever I'm around Mrs. Fields. I love her accent, plus she's always cheery and upbeat. Not to say Mr. Fields isn't; he's just more chill about it. Felix is a perfect mix of them. Speaking of Mr. Fields . . .

"Where's your dad?" I ask Felix. Normally, when you see one Fields, you see 'em all.

"He's gonna meet us there," Felix says. "Him and Grandma gotta get food from the restaurant."

"Pans and pans of peas and rice!" Mrs. Fields adds. My stomach rumbles just thinking about it.

"Zo Zo, you didn't say hi to me!" whines Connie.

I turn around to where Felix's little brother and sister are sitting. Connie's seven and Allan is six.

"Hey, guys!" I say. I always tell Felix he's lucky to be the oldest, but he doesn't see it that way. "Awww, you guys are so cute!"

"Cute?" Allan wrinkles his nose. He has on a coat, but I can tell he's wearing a suit underneath; probably a bow tie, too, since he's into those.

"Sorry," I tell him. *"Handsome?"*

"Nah, I'm Gucci!" Allan says, grinning with his two front teeth missing.

"Allan, watch your mouth!" Mrs. Fields scolds from the front. "Felix, where he hear that from?"

"Mom," Felix sighs, "Gucci is not a bad word."

"Well, it doesn't sound proper," Mrs. Fields says.

Felix shakes his head and I snicker under my breath. Mrs. Fields is funny like that.

"Wanna see my signs?" I ask Felix, unraveling them before he can answer. I made them last night before going to bed and plan to hang them from my selling table. In my book bag I have tape, a stapler, an orange pencil case

41

for holding the cash I'll get, and one of those cheap plastic tablecloths, compliments of Palace Farms. I also have a folder with my fundraiser packet and Felix's, since he clearly won't need it.

"Nice," Felix says, studying the signs. I wrote *Support Kentwood Kids!* on them and decorated with flowers, butterflies, and, well, cookies.

"Got three sales already," I tell him. "Mom got peanut butter, Daddy got the classic chocolate chip, and Mark got the M&M ones."

"You got Mark to buy some?" Felix asks. He's been around long enough to know that every extra penny Mark gets goes toward his musical equipment. Literally. He'll pick up pennies and nickels off the ground.

"Of course," I say. I don't mention that I had to agree to fold his laundry for a week.

"Felix tells me I gotta buy cookie dough from you, Zoe." Mrs. Fields smiles at me in the rearview mirror. "You're going for something big, yah?"

"Yes," I tell her. "I kinda have a big sales goal."

"Well, spunky girl like you, I just know you'll make it," Mrs. Fields says. "Put me down for the macadamia nut ones."

"Okay!" I immediately reach down into my bag and get my order form. "How many tubs do you want? Regular size is nine dollars, and jumbo size is twelve dollars."

Felix nudges me. I shrug and mouth, "What?" Just trying to get my sale.

"I'll talk to Delbert and let ya know," Mrs. Fields says. "Those are his favorite."

We get to the church a few minutes later, and I can't believe how full the parking lot is. Inside the lobby, we meet up with Mr. Fields and Felix's grandma, who squeezes tight when she hugs me.

"Good to see you, sweetie!" she says.

"Hey, Zoe girl," Mr. Fields says, holding out his hand. "You here to take all our money, eh?"

"No," I laugh, giving him a high five. "I'm here for youth day."

I ignore the face Felix is making and follow everyone inside the sanctuary. We find an empty row and settle in. A girl in the row in front of us immediately turns around and smiles.

"Hey, Felix," she says. Felix cheeses extra hard. Hmm-mmm.

"W'sup, Ny'rai?" he says.

"You staying for the potluck?" she asks.

"Yep. You?"

Ny'rai nods and lowers her voice.

"I wish we could skip everything and get right to the food!"

Felix grins.

"Yeah."

"Ah-heeemmmm!" I fake a cough and bump Felix's arm as I go to cover my mouth.

"Oh, this is my friend Zoe," Felix says, snapping out of it. "Zoe, this is Ny'rai."

"Hey, Zoe," Ny'rai says.

"Hello." I smile at her, but I'm not so sure about this girl.

"Do you go to Kentwood?" Ny'rai asks me.

"Yeah," I say. Has Felix talked to her about me? Should I even care?

"Ny'rai goes to Excelsior," Felix tells me. Am I supposed to be impressed?

"Well, that's excellent," I say. For some reason, I feel like Mr. Boyd. Yuck!

"All right, now, young people." Mr. Fields leans over and clears his throat, our cue to be quiet. Ny'rai grins at Felix again and turns around. Everyone claps as the music starts and a group of people grab microphones and begin to sing. I sweep this Ny'rai girl from my mind and enjoy the songs. Maybe Mark should've come with me, so he could experience a *real* band!

Kids of all ages lead the program. They sing, pray, dance, and even recite poetry, which is pretty cool. While a tall guy with glasses talks about a story from the Bible, I can't keep my mind still. I grab my idea notebook and jot down my article ideas. *"Kids in charge: Would it really be so bad?" "How to spot fake friends." "Why does music make us feel good?"*

Once I'm done with my ideas, I let my eyes wander around the church. There's a good number of people in here. I start counting, which is kind of hard to do without anyone noticing.

"What are you doing?" Felix whispers when I lean over him a tiny bit.

"Nothing!" I return-whisper.

I estimate 124 people. One hundred and twenty-four! If even half the people here buy a tub of cookie dough, I'm over the fifty-item requirement! Before the pastor says the final amen, I am pumped!

"You don't wanna eat first?" Felix asks as I basically drag him toward the lobby doors.

"No, I gotta get set up," I tell him. "Which way to the basement?"

"You're obsessed," Felix says, but he leads the way to the stairs and helps me pull a small table to the entrance of the dining area. I spread out my yellow tablecloth (because yellow equals happiness), arrange my flyers and order forms, and practice my sales pitch. Most people have been hanging around upstairs talking, but hunger must be getting the best of them, because more people trickle inside and grab seats at the tables.

"Hello, young lady; hello, Felix," says an older couple.

"Hi, Mr. and Mrs. Patrick," Felix says.

"Hi, I'm Zoe!" I say with a megawatt smile. "I go to school with Felix, and our school is selling cookie dough to raise money for field trips and valuable after-school clubs. I'm positive we have one of your favorites here."

I hand the lady the cookie dough brochure, and she immediately locks in on the double chocolate chip picture.

"Lord knows I don't need this!" she says, flipping through the rest of the list.

"Well, it *is* for a good cause," I say. "Maybe for the grandkids?"

"Oh, it'll be all for her," Mr. Patrick says with a laugh, patting his wife's arm. "Just order what you want, dear. I'll get you a plate."

After a few more words of encouragement, Mrs. Patrick orders two tubs of cookie dough, and I have five total orders.

"Only ninety percent to go!" says Felix. I stare at him and he laughs. "That's why you should pay attention in math."

Whatever.

I get a few more sales using the same method. Felix says hello to people he knows, then I go in with the charm, introducing myself and tempting them with pictures of mouthwatering cookies. But before long, I lose Felix to two things: food and Ny'rai.

As soon as she walks into the dining area and waves to Felix, I know he's done.

"Line's getting long," he tells me. "Let's get some food."

"You go ahead," I say. "I'll get sales while people are waiting."

He's gone before I'm finished with my sentence. I think that article idea about spotting fake friends is a winner.

I take a deep breath, come from behind the table, and start passing out the cookie brochures to people in line.

"Hi, everyone! While you wait for a plate of delicious food, you can support the students of Kentwood Academy *and* satisfy your sweet tooth, too! We have something for everyone, and orders will be personally delivered to your homes. Stop by my table anytime!"

I hear lots of "oooh"s and "ahhhh"s as people flip through the pictures, but no one stampedes my table. I think everyone's more interested in getting a plate. I can see the serving table, and the food does look good. That's okay, though; I can wait.

"Horizon WordPro . . . Horizon WordPro," I tell myself.

"You gonna eat, sweetie?" Felix's grandmother is walking to her seat with a plate of steaming food. I stare too

47

long at the greens, rice and peas, fried chicken, macaroni and cheese, and sweet potatoes.

"Ummm, yes, ma'am," I say. "Just want to be here in case someone comes to order."

"Dedicated girl, but don't wait too long; food's moving fast!" she warns.

She winks at me and walks to her table, leaving tempting smells behind. I scan the room for Felix, but he's already sitting down with his plate. Ny'rai's at the table with him, along with some other kids I don't know. As I watch, I wonder something. Since Felix does so many things, does he have different sets of friends? Like, school friends, church friends, swim friends, track and field friends? Watching him laugh with the kids at the table makes me also wonder, am I his *best* friend?

The brown teddy bear on my bed at home definitely says I am, but I wonder if it still counts, since he gave it to me in third grade. Felix was real close to his other grandma, his mom's mom, back then. When she passed away, it was the first and only time I saw Felix cry. I didn't like it. So when our grandparents' day program rolled around a few weeks later, I did my best to dress up like Nanny Jean so Felix wouldn't be so sad. Even though other kids were laughing, Felix loved it. And the next day he gave me the Best Friends Forever bear. It's been true so far.

"So, you must be the cookie lady."

I blink away the Felix memories and turn on my Zoe Mode and give the gray-haired man in front of me a smile.

"Yes, sir! I'm Zoe, and I'm selling cookie dough for Kentwood Academy."

"Well, you don't have to go through your whole speech, I already see what I want. Classic chocolate chip, jumbo size."

"Excellent choice!" I tell the man, recognizing him as the pastor. "I'll just need you to write your information on this order form. I'll be personally delivering your delicious cookie dough."

He writes down his address and phone number and hands me a ten-dollar bill and two ones.

"Come back and visit us anytime, Miss Zoe," he says.

"I will!"

Two more people place orders before sales slow waaaay down. My stomach is growling up a storm, but I don't want to give up and miss a customer.

"Here," Felix says, handing me a cup of punch. "How'd it go?"

I fight the urge to say something snarky to him about his disappearing act, and gulp down the sweet and fizzy drink before answering.

"Good," I say.

Felix grabs the order form.

"Wow, thirteen tubs sold," he says. "Nice start."

"Maybe Ny'rai wants to buy some," I say.

"She said she would ask her mom," Felix says. "Anyway, my mom made you a plate."

"Cool," I say. At least *somebody* thought about me.

Felix's mom brings the plate a few seconds later, and she has a lady with her.

"Even the best salesladies need food!" Mrs. Fields says. "And I got one more customer for you."

"Hi, Zoe, nice to meet you," the lady says. "I'm Mrs. Butler, and I think you've already met my daughter."

Like magic, Ny'rai appears at her mother's side.

"Yes, I did." I paste on my smile. "Thanks for supporting Kentwood; I know Ny'rai goes to a different school."

"Of course!" Mrs. Butler says. "Felix was telling us about your goal. It's so nice to see a young person with such ambition."

"Thank you!"

"Mrs. Butler runs the kids' group that Felix and Ny'rai are a part of," Mrs. Fields says. "Maybe you'd be interested in joining."

"Oh, um, maybe," I say, caught off guard. "I'll ask my mom."

Mrs. Butler nods and tells Ny'rai to pick two tubs of cookies.

"We're gonna be leaving soon, Zoe," Mrs. Fields says. "Why don't you wrap up and eat."

I nod, taking the plate from her hands.

"Felix! Help with the chairs," Mrs. Fields calls to him.

I pack my stuff up and attack the plate. Everything starts off delicious, but then a funny thing happens. As I watch Felix, Ny'rai, and the other kids help the grown-ups stack chairs and clean off the tables, the food doesn't taste so good anymore. I know it's silly, but I feel like Felix should be *my* friend only, not shared with anybody else.

But I guess he's not.

I swallow hard and make myself go into Zoe Mode. I tell myself that once I reach my fifty sales—no, once I go *over* fifty sales—Felix will see who the best friend really is.

Chapter 6

At the Top

I get to school a few minutes before first bell for once, and I'm feeling good. I had a lovely egg-and-cheese breakfast sandwich, courtesy of Mom, and I got to eat it while watching Miss Douglas's morning news segment. To top it off, the car started up just fine, and Daddy actually let me listen to *my* music!

It feels weird not to visit Ms. Hamilton first thing, and I hurry to Mr. Boyd's classroom before my luck changes. The breakfast sandwich almost comes back up when I see Amaya already there. Miss Douglas told us our homeroom teachers would be tracking sales every Monday, and I've been worried all weekend about how many tubs of cookie dough Amaya sold. I had a nightmare on Saturday night that she really did sell fifty. On Sunday, I begged Daddy to take my order form with him to work.

"Zoe, I'm not sure that's within company policy for me to do," he said at first. But, of course, I didn't give up.

"You don't have to ask everybody," I told him, though it would be great if he did. "Just people you're close with."

I started naming some of his coworkers who I know and reminding him of how they always love to see me, blah blah blah, until he crumbled. Good thing he did, though, because he came home with seven orders.

But now, as Amaya gives me a smug smile, I wonder if my twenty-two orders are enough to beat her.

"Zoe, how was the weekend?" asks Mr. Boyd in his robot voice.

"Wonderful," I tell him, plopping onto my seat. "Yours?"

"Not bad at all," he says.

"Hey, Zoe," Felix says, coming into the classroom a second later.

"Hey," I tell him. Still not sure why I'm feeling some kind of way toward him.

"How'd it go yesterday?" he asks. "Any more sales?"

"Yeah, Zoe, any more sales?" Amaya's mocking voice and laugh make me clench my fists.

"Felix," I say with attitude, "I'll answer your question when Miss Nosy decides to mind her own business."

The bell rings and Felix walks to his seat, his face kinda scrunched up like he's confused. I mean, I wasn't trying to take anything out on him. I'm just so sick of Amaya. He should know that.

"Before we get to math, I want to focus your attention on our handy-dandy dough chart," Mr. Boyd says. He has a poster board on an easel, decorated all cheesy, with the Kentwood Hornets logo at the very top. *Week 1, Week 2,* and *Week 3* are written on the left side of the poster, and the words *GRAND TOTAL* are in bold at the bottom.

"Now, I'm sure a few of you know that I can be quite competitive," Mr. Boyd says. "So I'd like nothing more than to be the winning classroom this year."

"What's in it for you?" asks a boy named Jeffrey Winston.

"Bragging rights," Mr. Boyd says. Something in his eyes lets me know he doesn't get those very often. Well, that's all about to change.

Mr. Boyd starts calling names, and kids say how many orders they got.

"First one to give me a total on these gets ten extra-credit points," he says as he writes our numbers.

Three must be the magic number, because that's how many tubs most kids have sold. A few even say zero, with sheepish grins.

I start strategizing when I notice that Mr. Boyd is calling names alphabetically. Shaw is before Sparks, so I'll get

54

to hear Amaya's number before having to say mine. What if hers is more than mine? I *cannot* watch her smug face if that happens. So I make a decision. If Amaya has more sales than me, I'll report a number that's higher than whatever she says and hustle hard to get that number for real. Probably not the most honest choice, but it'll have to work.

"Amaya?" Mr. Boyd asks. I clench my fists. *This is it.* . . .

"Eighteen," Amaya says proudly. My mouth drops open. A bunch of "whoa!"s and "dang!"s float across the classroom. And yeah, compared to twos and threes, eighteen sounds amazing.

"Impressive!" Mr. Boyd says, adding her number to the list.

"Erin?"

"One."

"Zoe?"

I don't answer right away, building up the right amount of anticipation.

"Twenty-two."

Mr. Boyd turns and raises an eyebrow.

"Twenty-two, Zoe? Wow, you really did have a wonderful weekend! This is incredible!"

He writes *22,* the last number of the list.

"Okay," Mr. Boyd says. "Now who can—"

"Eighty-two."

Felix gives the answer to our class total so far. Like he needs the extra credit.

Later, while we work in groups during science, Amaya turns to me smugly and asks, "Be honest; you didn't *really* sell that many, did you?"

"Yeah, I did, Amaya," I tell her. "Get over it."

"Oh, I already am," Amaya says. "I barely went through half my neighborhood, and, duh, I couldn't go to my dad's job over the weekend."

"Whatever."

Amaya leaves me alone for the moment, but I can't help thinking about what she said. She lives in one of those fancy neighborhoods where you have to punch in a code to get in, kinda like the Whitfields'. I only know because she invited our whole third-grade class to her birthday party once. If she got eighteen orders by only going through half her neighborhood, who knows where she'll be after a whole week! My dad only got seven orders at his job; I'm sure her dad could get a hundred. I try to turn on my Zoe Mode, but it's super hard to now.

The next part of Felix's plan is to sell in my neighborhood, going door-to-door like Amaya did. But will that be enough? What I really need is a neighborhood like Amaya's.

And that's when I get a genius idea of my own.

I forget all about my detention until I'm putting my fund-raiser folder into my backpack after lunch and see the crumpled slip of paper.

"Maaannn," I sigh. This wrecks my plan. Gotta find Felix!

"Hey, you have anything after school today?" I say, after finding him at his locker.

"Huh?"

"I have a stupid detention so I can't leave right after."

"Oh." Felix frowns. "I have swim practice at the Aquatic Center, so Mom'll be here at three-thirty on the dot."

"Ugh!" One little thing sometimes changes everything. *Think, Zoe, think!*

"Can I borrow your phone?" I ask Felix.

"Uh, no," Felix says. "We're not supposed to have phones during the day."

"Felix, come on! It's lunchtime!"

"Nah, Zoe. I'm not getting it taken away."

The lunch bell rings and the hall starts filling up.

"Please? I'll be super-fast. I gotta find a ride home, re-member? And you know I have no data and the stingy school won't let us connect to their Wi-Fi!"

Felix sighs but reaches in his bag and hands me his phone.

"Hurry up," he says, glancing around.

I go to his text app and type in Mark's number.

> Mark, it's Zoe. Can you come get me at 4:30?
>
> Have detention 😿

I guess high school has different rules about cell phones, because Mark texts back in a few seconds.

> SMH, wat u do this time?

I hate when people don't answer my original question.

> NOTHING! Was late. Can u get me????

"Zoe, hurry up," Felix says.

"Okay, okay," I tell him, waiting for Mark's response.

> Yeah

Perfect!! One little thing changes everything, I guess. Mark picking me up actually makes my plan even better. So glad I remembered that he has Mom's car today!

"Thanks, Fe Fe," I say, handing Felix his phone. He snatches it and glares at me.

"Stop calling me that," he says, closing his messaging app.

"Excuse me, young man, why are you on your cell phone?"

Felix jumps. Mr. Grayson, one of the safety monitors, frowns at him.

"Oh, no worries, sir," I tell him. "I needed to use his phone to get a ride home."

I decide not to mention the detention part and flash Mr. Grayson a big smile.

"If a student needs to call home, he or she should use the office phone," Mr. Grayson tells us.

"Yes, sir, we will!" I say, tugging Felix's arm. "C'mon, we're gonna be late to class."

Felix barely gets his locker closed before I drag him down the hall.

"Hurry up!" I hiss. "He's, like, two seconds from taking your phone!"

We make it to Mr. Boyd's classroom and I breathe a sigh of relief.

"See? Sometimes you just gotta smile big and talk fast!" I tell Felix. He's not smiling like I am.

"I knew I shouldn't have let you use my phone," he says.

"He didn't take it, Felix," I tell him. "Relax!"

Felix just walks away from me. Dang, is he *really* that upset?

Yeah, he is.

For the rest of the day, anytime I try to talk or joke with him, he acts bored or gives one-word answers. It definitely doesn't feel great, but I can't worry about it right now. I gotta stay focused on my goal.

Detention drags on, but to my surprise, Mark is waiting outside when I'm finally released from prison.

"Wow, Zoe" is all he says.

"What? You know how the parents are in the morning."

Mark shakes his head as he leaves the pickup area.

"Soooo," I say, jumping into my plan. "You have practice today?"

"Yeah." Mark eyes me suspiciously. "Why?"

"Can I go with you?"

"Why, Zoe?"

"The computer disaster. Duh!"

I don't know why I don't just tell Mark the real reason. I guess the computer excuse sounds better.

"I'll just take you to the lib—"

"No!"

I'm louder than I thought, and Mark makes a face. I take a deep breath.

"I mean, it's easier at Chad's house. Plus, did I tell you the CRIM inspired one of my articles?"

"Yeah, whatever," Mark says.

"I'm serious! I'll share the doc with you once we get there."

"Look, you don't need to be tagging along with me to practice all the time."

"Oh, trust me," I tell him. "In three weeks, you won't even see me anymore."

We stop home for Mark's guitar stuff, and I change from my slightly grimy school jacket into my fancy, special-occasions coat. Mark watches me as he devours a container of yogurt and a banana.

"You betta not bug me about being ready to leave," Mark warns.

"I won't, I won't." I give him the megawatt smile and throw in some extra blinking.

"Something's wrong with you," Mark says.

I pay attention to everything once we get into Chad's neighborhood. His house is in a cul-de-sac, and I count thirteen houses on his street. That's a good start.

I help Mark carry his stuff inside and the jokes start immediately.

"Awww! You brought the li'l roadie again, huh?" Chad teases.

"Ha ha," I say. "You won't be laughing when I'm famous."

"Yeah, cuz I'll be too old to laugh by then!" Chad replies, messing with my hair.

"Whatever!" I say, smacking his hand away.

"Beanie's running late," Rodney says, reading a message on his phone.

"What else is new?" says Mark.

"Here's something new," Chad says with a grin. "The folks are at some event at the university, so we can jam as long as we need to."

"Bet!" says Rodney. "Let's get it!"

"You need the computer, Zo Zo?" Chad asks.

"No—I mean, yes," I say, almost blowing my own cover. Things could not be better for me, though, cuz now I don't have to tell Mrs. Whitfield I need to go outside for some air.

"Well, once you figure it out, you know where to go!"

Chad tugs my puff and my head jerks to the side. Apparently, this is super hilarious. Beanie shows up a few minutes later and the guys head downstairs. I walk up to the loft of glory. I'm thinking I should at least turn the computer on and pretend to be working on something. I open a doc and type a headline. *Participation trophies: Are they ruining good ol' competition?* Problem is, once I start writing, words just flow and it's hard to stop. I'm almost to the bottom of the first page when I remember why I'm really here. I close my document and tiptoe downstairs. Honestly, I could stomp down each and every step and nobody would hear me, as loud as the CRIM is.

It's chilly outside, but my Zoe Mode won't let a little

winter stop me. I've got my pencil case/money carrier in my bag, and I'm gripping a clipboard that I swiped from Daddy. I figure it'll be easier to start at the end of the block and work my way over to Chad's house. That way, I'll be able to see if his parents come home.

Nobody's at the first house I go to, but I hit the jackpot at the second house: five orders! The lady who answers the door says she's having a party next month and now she won't have to worry about dessert.

"A little brisk to be outside, isn't it, dear?" says the man who answers the door at the third house.

"Yes, sir, it is, but I'm really committed to my school," I answer with a smile.

"I can't say no to that!" he says. He calls his wife. "Helen! What kind of cookies do you want?"

Two more orders!

Houses four and five say "no thank you," and house six orders a jumbo tub of chocolate toffee crunch. By the time I get back to Chad's house, I've sold twelve tubs of cookie dough. I'm safely sitting in the loft at the computer when the Whitfields get home and flicker the lights for the CRIM. Of course, I turn on the magic for them and get three more sales.

"You're doing too much, Zoe," Mark says on the ride home. He's all irritated that I hit up the Whitfields and the CRIM for sales.

"You mean selling too much?" I counter. "Yes, I am."

"You need to chill out sometimes," he says. "It can be annoying."

"As annoying as your band?" I ask.

"Wow, that's the best you got, Miss Writer?"

Neither of us says anything for a while. Mark of all people should know what it's like to go after something you want. So why's he giving me a hard time? Matter of fact, it seems like *everyone* in my family is giving me a hard time about the fundraiser. Daddy barely wanted to take my packet to work, and Mom acted like getting twenty-two orders was enough, that I didn't need to sell anymore. Maybe they're all just mad that I'm getting this done without them. Maybe the power of Zoe Mode is too much for them. Well, too bad! Because once Zoe Mode is activated, there's no stopping me!

Chapter 7

The Sale Next Door

Since selling went so well in Chad's neighborhood yesterday, I decide to try selling in my own today. We know our neighbors mostly by the whole waving/"How're you doing" thing, so I start with the five houses where I know people's actual names.

"Hi, Mr. Logan, how are you?" I ask when the first neighbor slowly pulls the door open. Mr. Logan's a pretty grumpy guy since his wife died, but he's always liked me. He says I have spunk just like his wife, Louise, did.

"Still breathin'," he grunts. "I'll tell you what, though; this cold air is whippin' right through to my bones, so make it snappy!"

O-kaaay, then.

"My school is doing a cookie dough fundraiser, to raise money for field trips and—"

"How much?" Mr. Logan interrupts, reaching in his pocket for his wallet.

"Well, regular size tubs are nine dollars, and the jumbo tubs are twelve dollars. Do you want to see our flavors?"

"No, no," Mr. Logan says, "I'd rather get back to my rocking chair and book, little miss. Why don't you pick the flavors for me, all right? Two regular tubs."

Mr. Logan hands me a twenty-dollar bill. I go to my pencil case to get his two dollars, but he's already closing the door.

"Keep the change, Sparky," he says.

I stand on his porch for a second to write down his address and order. Hmm, what kind of cookies would Mr. Logan like? I take a chance and pick the sugar cookies and the lemon drops before moving on to the next house.

The Taylors have, like, five kids, so they'll probably either want a ton of cookies or absolutely none at all.

"Hey, Zoe." Mrs. Taylor answers the door with a kid in a diaper on her hip. I can hear pounding footsteps behind her, and soon two more kids appear.

"Hi, Mrs. Taylor," I say. "Would you guys be interested in buying some cookie dough to support Kentwood Academy?"

"COOKIES!"

"Mommy, I want the cookies!"

Yikes, maybe this wasn't a good idea after all. Mrs.

Taylor looks super-annoyed, and I feel like she's gonna slam the door in my face.

"No, not today, Zoe," she says, hoisting up the diapered kid, who's saying his own version of "Cookie!"

One of the kids on the ground tries to convince her.

"But we want cookies! Buy some, Mommy!"

"I said no!" Mrs. Taylor says firmly.

"Awww!" The kids whine, but Mrs. Taylor gives them a look and they scurry away.

"Well, if you change your mind, just stop by my house, okay?" I say. "We're selling for three weeks and have a really great variety."

"Thanks, Zoe, I'll keep that in mind." Mrs. Taylor gives me a smile, so I flash her the megawatt, wave, and bounce down her steps like I'm not disappointed at all.

The Wheelers aren't home, and Mrs. Armstrong tells me she's diabetic and doesn't need the sugar.

"Y'all should be selling veggie platters or reduced-price Edible Arrangements," she says. "You got any of that?"

"No," I say, "but I'll ask about it for our next fundraiser."

"All right, then, don't stay in this cold for long!"

I sigh once she closes her door. Don't these people realize that only a serious person braves the frigid cold to sell cookie dough? Well, closed doors and cold weather won't get to Zoe Sparks! I'm gonna go to every house on my block, and then I'll walk to the next block and go to every house there, too! In fact, I guarantee that I'll have some fantastic article ideas from being out here.

Five houses later, my fingers feel like icicles and my teeth are chattering so much, I can't even get through my cookie dough speech. I trudge back home to warm up. When I get there, both Mom and Daddy are home and sitting at the kitchen table with a notepad and papers all over the place.

"Brrrrrrr!" I say when nobody notices me. Mom finally looks over. Talk about being invisible!

"Zoe, were you outside all this time?"

"Duty calls, so Zoe answers," I say, pumping my fist. No one smiles.

"It's pretty cold today," Daddy says, studying a piece of paper in front of him.

"I know," I say, blowing on my hands. "That's why I came in to warm up."

I sit down and put my order form and pencil case on the table. Daddy sighs, like he'd really prefer that I do this somewhere else.

Three sales from today, plus fifteen from yesterday, plus—

"Zoe, it's probably not a good idea to be carrying that much money around," Mom says, eyeing my pencil case, which is full of checks, cash, and coins.

"Okay," I say. "I'll empty it before I hit the streets again."

"Go back out?" Daddy finally looks up. "I don't think so."

"Why not?" I ask. "I only got three orders, and I need to check the houses where people weren't home yet."

"Zoe, it's cold and it's getting dark. I think it's a wrap for today," Daddy says. "And I think you might be taking this fundraiser thing a bit too far."

Ugh!

"You know," I say, flashing him a smile and wiggling my eyebrows, "if you guys just decide to buy me the WordPro, all this selling could be done—right here, right now."

"As usual, your timing is terrible, Zoe," Daddy says with a frown. He picks up another piece of paper.

I sit perfectly still, feeling cold and small. Daddy usually at least smiles at my charming ideas and comments. Lately, he's been shooting me down pretty hard.

"Sweetie, do you have homework?" Mom asks. Guess this is *her* way of dismissing me.

"Yeah," I say, even though I don't. I'm not excited about sticking around them, either.

"Why don't you get working on it," Mom says. "I'll be starting dinner soon. Chicken noodle soup."

I get my stuff and stand up from the table without saying anything else. I keep my coat and hat on in my room until I warm up. Since I don't have homework, I decide to run myself a bubble bath. I fill the tub with so much water, I have to be very still or it'll slosh over the side. I breathe in the citrus smell of the bubbles and reread my latest *WriteOn!* magazine. When Mom calls me for dinner, I make sure to stay in for ten extra minutes.

Chapter 8

Hustle and Dough

Felix is back to normal today, which is a good thing, because I could really use his help. So at lunch, after he tells me something funny that happened at Mango Bay yesterday, I do something that I really hate doing.

"Sorry about the cell phone thing, Felix," I tell him. I make sure not to add that if I hadn't been so quick thinking, Mr. Grayson probably would have had it taken away.

Felix pretends to be shocked.

"Wow, the world must be ending," he says.

"Stop it!" I smack his arm. "I'm serious!"

"Oww!" He rubs the spot. "You gonna apologize for that, too?"

"You deserved that," I tell him. "But for real, are we good?"

"Yeah, we good," Felix says. I would never tell him this,

but I feel relieved to hear him say it. A Felix-less life would be, well, Felix-less.

"So, are you coming to my meet today?" he asks. "Mom said you can ride with us."

"Ummm, yeah?"

"You forgot, didn't you?" Felix crosses his arms and stares at me.

"No," I lie. *Think fast, think fast!* "I was just hoping we wouldn't have to miss Journalism Club."

"Oh." Felix dunks a french fry into a mound of ketchup. "Well, I gotta be there at five, so we should be okay."

"Cool."

Truth is, I would rather come up with more sales ideas than watch Felix swim. It's nothing personal; I just hate wasting time when the stakes are so high! But since me and him are all good now, I can't *not* go.

"That reminds me"—Felix pats his camera, which is sitting on the table beside his tray—"I gotta take a few pictures."

Miss Douglas actually liked my school lunch idea, but she said we have to do things in a "decent" way; no throwing people under the bus or biased complaining. Miss Douglas said that sometimes, if you highlight somebody in a positive light, they start living up to it. She thinks we might have success with our school-lunch issues if we try things this way.

"Get a shot of them serving food," I suggest. "One where somebody is smiling."

"That might be harder than you think," Felix says, watching the lunch line. "But the King is on it!"

Felix takes a giant bite of his cheeseburger.

"It's really not that bad," he says, mouth half-open.

"Ewww, chew with your mouth closed!" I say.

While Felix walks around snapping pictures, I take the bun off my burger and examine what's underneath. There's no way I can afford to get food poisoning right now, not with everything I have on my plate (pun intended).

"What are you looking for—your brain?"

I turn to see Amaya walking by with her empty tray, the usual smirk on her face.

"Not something I have to search for," I say. "Let me know when you find yours."

"I'll email you," Amaya says over her shoulder, "from my new WordPro."

I freeze. Maybe it's the way Amaya says the word *new,* but something hits me. She doesn't even *need* a Horizon WordPro; she probably already has one! Maybe two! She's only doing this so *I* don't get one! I watch her walk away, like this is all a game. *It is so on!*

"Uh-oh, your face is all Zoe Mode. We definitely don't want that as a picture," Felix says. He puts down his camera, which was pointed at me a second ago.

"You okay?" he asks.

"Yeah, fine," I say.

"You gonna eat that?" Felix nods at my burger.

"That's gonna be a no," I tell him. My appetite is officially gone.

Felix attacks my burger while I nibble at my apple slices.

"How well do you know your neighbors?" I ask Felix.

"Huh?"

"Do you guys, you know, talk to your neighbors?" I ask. Felix's family lives in an apartment building, but I figure they gotta know at least some of their neighbors.

"Not really." Felix shrugs and starts in on his fries again. "Why?"

"I don't know; maybe some of them like cookies?"

"You wanna sell at my place?"

"I mean, sure, sounds good to me."

"I wasn't inviting you to, I was just—" Felix tries to explain, but I cut him off.

"Can I use your phone to see if my dad can pick me up from your house?"

Felix opens his mouth to shut me down, but I flash him a smile.

"Just kidding!"

We end up having to leave Journalism Club a little early because Mrs. Fields is worried about us running into traffic on the way.

"Such a big event!" Mrs. Fields says when we pull into the packed parking lot at the Aquatic Center.

"You nervous?" I ask Felix.

He looks up from his phone like he's just realizing we've arrived.

"Nope."

"Pride goes before a fall, Felix," Mrs. Fields says.

"You mean a dive?" Felix says with a smug grin. Mrs. Fields tries to give Felix *the look,* but I see her lips struggling not to twist up into a smile.

Once we're inside the center, I realize two things Felix didn't tell me about swim meets: (1) They're crowded, and the seats are uncomfortable bleacher-style. (2) They're long and boring.

We sit there for close to an hour before Felix even swims. And it's not like he can talk to us during the wait; the bleachers where we're sitting are up on the second floor!

Mrs. Fields cheers him on (loudly) the second he hits the water. I can't lie; Felix is fast, like a dolphin. I'm impressed but not surprised when he comes in first.

"That's my boy!!" Mrs. Fields yells. I yell right along with her.

"He's got two more events," Mrs. Fields tells me. "Wait till you see his relay team in action!" She claps her hands together to demonstrate the speed.

"So, um, how long do these things usually go?" I ask.

"Couple hours," Mrs. Fields says, like it's nothing. "Maybe three."

My mouth drops open, and Mrs. Fields chuckles.

"I know, sweetie," she says. "He didn't tell me the first time either."

Mrs. Fields offers to buy me a slice of pizza, which I say yes to. While she's gone, I watch some other kids swim. Why did I ever say I would come to this?

"Hey, Zoe!"

Amari's mom, Mrs. Myers, waves to me on her way to her seat a few rows behind me.

"Hi, Mrs. Myers," I say. "I didn't know Amari was a swimmer."

"Yep, he's our resident fish," she says with a laugh.

"Well, you definitely came prepared," I say. She has a book under her arm, a container of nachos, a water bottle, and a pack of cookies.

"I've learned my lesson," she says. "First time for you?"

"Yeah, I'm here with Felix," I say.

"Enjoy!" she tells me.

"You, too."

"I would so much more if these were warm and fresh from the oven," Mrs. Myers jokes, shaking her bag of cookies. I watch her climb up to her seat and the light bulb goes off in my head.

"Mrs. Myers!" I call, grabbing my stuff and following her. "If warm, fresh cookies are your thing, we need to talk."

I whip out my order form and brochure.

"I'm pretty sure I have your flavor," I tell her with a smile.

"Oh, I already know you do," Mrs. Myers says. "Amari brought this home and hit us all up for orders already. Sorry, girl."

"Oh. It's okay."

I wasn't expecting her to say no. I feel dumb for even asking, because, duh! Of course Amari would've brought it home.

"Can I take a look?" the lady beside Mrs. Myers asks.

"Sure," I say, handing her the brochure. "Chocolate chip is always a classic, but we have other awesome flavors."

The lady asks if I take checks and orders two tubs. Then she passes the brochure to the lady next to her, who orders a tub, too! I scoot down and give my spiel to a group of people who have that *I love cookies* vibe.

"Now this is what I miss most about my kids being in school," says a grandma-looking lady. "Overpriced goodies!"

The people around her chuckle, but I get a few more sales.

"And you'll deliver these, dear, or will I need to pick up from your school?"

"I deliver," I say.

I scoot down to another section and pass my brochures around. A guy is practically drooling over the peanut butter cookies but acts like he can't order anything without his wife, who's at the bottom of the bleachers cheering for their daughter. I'm turning up the heat on closing the deal when I hear Mrs. Fields yelling.

"GO, FEEEELIX!!!"

I turn my attention to the pool, where Felix is finishing first in a race.

"I'll be down here if you decide," I tell the man and hurry down next to Mrs. Fields.

"He won again!" she tells me, her face full of a smile.

"I saw; it was awesome!" I tell her.

Mrs. Fields hands me a napkin-covered plate.

"Probably cold now, chile," she says. "You're quite the saleslady, eh?"

"Me? Um, I guess."

I feel a little bad that I missed some of the meet because I was busy making sales. But then I tell myself it's not like it's a basketball game, where Felix would always be in action.

When Felix climbs from the water, he scans the balcony,

looking for us. Mrs. Fields and I yell his name and wave. I can see his smile from here.

But on the way home, Felix is pretty quiet, considering he'll be competing in the state championship next week.

"Wait till we tell your dad!" Mrs. Fields says proudly, for the second time.

"You did great, Felix," I tell him, for the first time. Felix frowns.

"You saw me?" he asks.

"What?" My face feels hot. "Yeah, I was there the whole time."

"Zoe made good use of the dead time, I'll tell ya that," Mrs. Fields says. "How many sales, Zo?"

Felix stares at me, but his face is blank.

"I think five," I say softly.

Mrs. Fields tells some story about how she used to sell necklaces at school back in Trinidad, but I watch Felix, who's looking out his window.

"Am I dropping you home, Zoe?" Mrs. Fields asks. I open my mouth to ask if it's too late to sell at their apartment complex, but then Felix finally looks at me. His face says the answer he wants me to give.

"Yes, ma'am," I tell her. "I'm going home."

Chapter 9

It's On

On Monday, the class literally applauds when Amaya announces that she's sold fifty tubs of cookie dough. I feel frozen in my seat.

"Fifty?! That's incredible, Amaya!" Mr. Boyd says, writing her number on the chart. "Team Boyd all the way!"

Erin Small, who's next, has sold eight tubs. My heart thumps in my chest as Mr. Boyd writes her number.

"And, Zoe, how many total sales?"

"Forty-six," I mumble.

"Excellent!" Mr. Boyd writes the number. "I see a few of you are on fire!"

It's a good number, but not good enough. It's not fifty. I don't dare turn around, because I can already feel Amaya's triumphant grin drilling holes in the back of my head.

Felix raises his hand to give our classroom's total sales. One hundred and fifty-one.

"If each of us sells ten things of cookie dough, we'll have two hundred and seventy," he adds.

"That's correct, Felix." Mr. Boyd seems so hyped about anything math related.

"Do I get *extra* extra credit?" Felix asks.

"Ha ha, very clever." Mr. Boyd wags his finger.

"Felix is right, though," Amaya says. "We each need to sell at least ten tubs. I live next door to Josiah Turner, in Ms. Parrish's class, and he told me they were at a hundred and thirty sales on Friday. Who knows where they are now? Some of us need to step up our game."

"Whatever," says a boy named Carlos. "You're just saying that cuz you already sold five *times* ten and now you can stop anytime you want!"

"I'm not stopping till it's over," Amaya says, "and I think if we all did our part, our classroom could be the winner."

"That's the spirit, Amaya," Mr. Boyd says. "I think we could win, too. Let's take some motivation from Zoe and Amaya, everyone!"

Mr. Boyd moves on with his lesson, but I'm stuck on the Team Boyd poster board.

Amaya. 50
Zoe. 46

Seeing the numbers gives me a headache and makes my stomach hurt. I worked so hard, but it wasn't enough. And for Amaya to beat me makes it even worse. Her parents can afford to buy her anything, but she's determined to take the one thing I want . . . the one thing I *need*.

"Earth to Zoe." Felix waves a hand in front of my face and scoots his chair close to mine. "You didn't hear Mr. Boyd say to find a partner?"

I shake my head. This whole sales count has me zoned out.

"Look"—Felix lowers his voice—"you still have a chance, you know. Top seller in the school gets the prize, remember? Amaya getting to fifty first doesn't matter."

I sigh. Felix is right, but I think about how I went from house to house in the cold and talked to complete strangers to rack up my sales. What else is there to do?

"You can come to my apartment and sell if you want," Felix offers. "Maybe over the weekend?"

"Really?" I ask hopefully. "I thought you were mad at me."

"Mad? Nah," says Felix. "I think you're turning into a monster about this selling thing, but I get it. Plus, you're probably the only one who can come close to beating Amaya."

I glance over at Amaya, who's flipping her braids over her shoulder and laughing with her math partner. I imagine that she's laughing at me. That's enough to activate my Zoe Mode. I open my idea notebook.

"Okay, so we sell at your apartment. What else? Maybe my dad will let me set up a table at the Palace, like the Girl Scouts do."

"Maybe," Felix says. Mr. Boyd walks by, and we start working on the assignment he gave us.

A little before lunch, Felix and I get passes to go to the cafeteria. I'm interviewing Marsha Lerner, one of the kitchen crew, for next week's Who's Buzzin' column. Miss Douglas is pretty much guaranteeing that our lunches will improve after we do this positive article. The rest of us are skeptical. Amaya said we'll probably end up with toenails in our food.

"I've never been back here before," I say as me and Felix go into the kitchen.

We spot Ms. Lerner directing two other workers by the ovens, and I wave. She nods toward us and motions that she'll be over in a minute. Everything looks neat and clean.

"I don't see any poison," Felix whispers, taking a few pictures. I nudge him hard because Ms. Lerner has started walking our way.

"How you kids doin'?" Ms. Lerner asks. She's not smiling, but she doesn't seem mad, either. Her voice is huskier than I thought it would be, but it reminds me of my aunt

Sharon, Daddy's oldest sister. It's the kind of voice that means business.

"Good," says Felix.

"Thanks for your time; we'll be quick," I say.

"Like I said before, as long as y'all don't mind walking and talking, we'll be fine." Ms. Lerner grabs a stack of trays and motions for us to follow her.

"So, how long have you worked at Kentwood?" I ask.

"This is my eighth year," she says. "I started when my youngest was in fifth grade. Now that knucklehead'll be graduating in four months!"

I can tell Ms. Lerner is pretty proud about that. She says her other two kids are in college, and she can't wait for her last one to follow them.

"What's your favorite thing about working here in the cafeteria?"

"Seeing you kids grow over the years and move on," Ms. Lerner says. "Knowing I'm helping to keep you healthy with good food."

Ms. Lerner says her kids inspired her to go to college, and she's about to graduate with a degree in hospitality. She says her goal is to be the food-service director for an entire school district.

"Me and my son graduate two weeks apart," she tells us, smiling big. "It doesn't get no better than that!"

I swallow hard. Here come the hard questions.

"Do you get to pick the food that's served for lunch?"

"Not in my current role, no. I prepare the menu they give me. I'll have more say in that once I'm a director."

"What do you think about kids complaining about the food?"

"Kids these days gonna complain about everything," Ms. Lerner says without missing a beat. "If a student has a real concern about the food, they can fill out one of our BuzzCards. My staff reviews them every afternoon. You'd be surprised at how empty that box usually is."

"What's a BuzzCard?" Felix asks.

"Don't tell me you've never seen our comment box," Ms. Lerner says. She motions for us to follow her to the lunchroom.

Sure enough, there's a box near the door and a stack of comment cards beside it.

"My guess is that there might be one, two cards in there. Most of the time, it's stuff like, 'Serve strawberry milk!' or 'Why do we have to have a salad bar?'" Ms. Lerner says with a chuckle.

"Maybe the Art Club can help you create a new display for this," I tell her. "So it pops a little more."

"So it pops, huh," Ms. Lerner says with a smile. "I'm open to that."

"Great!" I say. "We should change the display every season, and maybe have a Café column in the paper. And you know how we have guest speakers to come in and talk to kids? What if we had a guest chef make lunch? Or if we had a battle of the cafeteria staff where kids judge the dishes?"

I know I'm rambling off a ton of ideas, but Ms. Lerner nods and even jots down some notes.

"I can't guarantee all of these," Ms. Lerner says, "but I definitely know where to come if I need new ideas!"

"I'm your girl!" I say with a huge smile.

"Well, I hate to rush you guys off, but lunch is about to start so I have to get to it," Ms. Lerner says.

"Thanks again for your time, Ms. Lerner," I say. Felix asks if he can get a quick picture of her stirring a pot in the kitchen. She says sure, and she actually smiles! So, since everyone's so happy, I go ahead and shoot my shot.

"Before we go, Ms. Lerner, the school is doing a cookie dough fundraiser. Are you interested in ordering some? Or maybe your staff?"

"No, ma'am." Ms. Lerner chuckles. "You're free to ask my staff after school, but my cookies are always from scratch. But I'm tickled that you asked me, and that you think I'm interesting enough to write an article on."

"Well, when you think about it, you feed the future!"

Ms. Lerner thanks us again, and we head to class.

"Unbelievable," Felix says, shaking his head as we walk

down the hallway. "You tried to sell cookies to the *kitchen crew?*"

"What?" I say. "Whatever it takes, right?"

"I guess," Felix says. He doesn't sound so sure. But after hearing Ms. Lerner's story, I'm more sure than ever.

Zoe Sparks will be the top cookie dough seller in the history of Kentwood Academy.

Chapter 10

Crown Down

"This is a really good article, Zoe," Miss Douglas says during Journalism Club on Wednesday. Not to brag or anything, but it's probably one of the best articles I've written; definitely a piece to use when applying for scholarships. I can see the headlines now: " 'Lunch with a lifelong Lerner' nets Zoe Sparks a full scholarship to wherever!"

"Your headline really captures the essence of the story," Miss Douglas continues. "Good work!"

"Thanks," I say. I can't keep the smile off my face. Combined with me *finally* getting to the fifty-order mark last night, things are looking good.

Miss Douglas moves around to Felix, and by the way he sits up straighter, he already knows what's coming.

"Felix, these pictures are amazing!" she says. "You two

really took what I said to heart. This is a very positive piece and gives us an inside view of one vital school employee."

"Did you notice her smile?" Felix asks, pointing at Ms. Lerner's face. "That was cuz of me."

"I'm sure it was." Miss Douglas pats Felix's shoulder before moving on to Amari and Erin, who cover sports.

"Show-off," I say, rolling my eyes.

"Whatever," Felix laughs, and makes his voice go all high, "Miss 'I got fifty sales! I got fifty sales!'"

"Shhhh!" I elbow him and peek around to see where Amaya is. She's far enough away where hopefully she can't hear us.

"I'm gonna beg my dad to let me sell at the Palace," I tell Felix. I don't mention that I've already asked and got shut down within a few seconds of my argument. I'm gonna go with the persistence route.

"What day are you going to the library?" he asks. That was another one of his ideas. I need to call each branch to see if I can come and set up a table to sell cookie dough. Felix says I should tell them the proceeds will help support literacy at Kentwood.

"Hopefully I can do a different branch every day," I tell him. "Only nine days left for the fundraiser!"

"Yeah, and I can't wait," Felix says, making a face. I

frown at him, but Miss Douglas starts talking about something before I can ask him what he means.

After our club meeting, Felix and I head outside to meet his mom.

"Isn't that your dad?" Felix asks. I'm shocked to see Daddy's Jeep parked behind Felix's mom's minivan.

"Yeah, it is," I say. "Guess I'm riding home with him."

"Good luck with your sales today," Felix says.

I just wave to him, already in Zoe Mode to convince Daddy this time.

"Hellooo, Daddy-o!" I say when I climb into the warm car.

"Hey, Zoe," he replies, definitely *not* as upbeat as I am. That's okay, I guess.

"So, it's actually great that you're picking me up today," I say. "Do you have to go to work now? Cuz if you do, I can come with you. Before you say no, just think about it. What do Girl Scouts really do, right? This fundraiser supports an actual school and—"

"ZOE!" Daddy's voice is sharp and louder than usual. He holds up his hand, and I stop mid-sentence. Daddy sighs. "Just give it a rest for a second, okay? I know this cookie dough sale is important to you, but it doesn't mean everyone else's world has to revolve around it."

Whoa . . . harsh! My eyes feel a little tingly, and I blink really fast. Why is Daddy being so mean? I cross my arms like a little kid—no, I don't care how silly I look—and shift toward my window. Daddy chuckles.

"I know you're not doing that again," he says. I don't answer.

"Come on, Zoe, snap out of that," Daddy says in a firm, I'm-being-nice-but-you-betta-do-it voice.

"I just don't see what the problem is!" I blurt. "You guys won't buy me the laptop, but when I try to get it myself, you won't let me do that, either!"

Daddy listens while I vent about Amaya and how she's able to get so many sales at *her* dad's job. By the time I'm finished, I notice that Daddy has pulled into one of those carport things at Sonic.

"The usual?" he asks. I nod.

"One medium side of tots and one large order of onion rings," Daddy orders. "And a large root beer and a large strawberry limeade with peach added."

"So, you have some stiff competition," Daddy says while we wait for our food. "I know what that's like."

"You don't know Amaya, Daddy," I say. "She's ruthless. Cutthroat."

Daddy laughs.

"All this in sixth grade?" he asks. "She sounds ready for the business world."

"I can't let her win," I say. "That's why I need to sell at your store."

The guy on skates comes with our order, and Daddy doesn't say anything until after he's had a few onion rings and a long sip of root beer.

"I can tell you now, Zo Zo, selling at Palace Farms isn't going to happen."

He holds up his hand before I can say anything.

"It's not gonna happen because I don't work there anymore."

"Wait . . . what? They fired you?" I almost drop my limeade. Those idiots fired my dad?

"Not exactly," Daddy says. "It's a layoff, which is a little different. That store is actually going to be closing, along with a few others in our area. Pretty soon the closest Palace Farms will be a few hours away."

"Why are they doing this?" I ask. "It's because of All-Foods, isn't it?"

I swear, they're taking over everything!!

Daddy laughs.

"You're so dramatic!" he says. "It's because of a lot of different things all put together."

"But you're the manager!" I say. "They can't do that!"

"It's already done," he says with a sigh.

"So that's why you're picking me up," I say. It starts to all come together for me, why Daddy has been so moody and why Mom has been working a lot more.

"Yep," Daddy says. "Not that I don't love picking you up, Queen Zoe."

"You haven't called me that in a while," I say. When I was little, he used to call me Queen Zoe and hand me one of the cardboard crowns from Palace Farms.

"You know what?" Daddy says, reaching to the back seat, where his green-and-gold Palace Farms messenger bag is. "Found this in my desk; couldn't bring myself to throw it away. For old times, I guess."

He smiles and hands me a gold crown. Any other time I would wrinkle my nose and tell him to stop being corny. But right now I take the crown and put it on. It feels perfect.

Chapter 11

#Goals

I think Daddy's job mojo is getting to me, cuz I haven't sold a single tub of cookie dough all day. We had a half day of school for teacher development or something, but I feel like the whole day has been a waste.

I'm sprawled on the couch, watching dance videos and eating cheesy popcorn. Mom's at work, and Daddy's somewhere "taking care of some business," whatever that means. Mark is upstairs in his room listening to music. Actually, it seems as if his music is getting louder by the minute, to the point where I can barely hear my show. This, of course, is normal for Mark, but for some reason, it really irritates me.

It also irritates me when the home phone rings and it's Felix.

"Yo yo, Zo Zo!" he says, cracking up at his own corniness. "Your cell not connected to the Wi-Fi?"

"Hey," I say, ignoring the shade he's throwing at my phone.

"Surprised you're not somewhere hustlin' somebody," Felix says.

"Don't feel like it today," I say with a yawn.

"What? You okay?"

"I'm fine."

"Well, you can come to the restaurant if you want," Felix offers. "Oh, and my championship meet is on Sunday at ten. Mom said you can ride with us again, unless your parents want to go."

"I'll ask," I say.

"Hey, if you don't wanna come, you don't have to," Felix says.

"No, I do," I say, but I know I don't sound too convincing. "I'll let you know if I need a ride."

"Okay," Felix says. "Well, I gotta go."

"Bye."

I toss the phone on the floor and turn the volume up on the TV. It sounds like Mark turns his volume up, too!

"Ugh!" I drag myself off the couch and stomp upstairs.

The vibe in our house has definitely been different since Daddy's layoff. Everyone's quieter (except for Mark), and we kinda just keep to ourselves. It's like no one wants to say the wrong thing; we're scared to be either too happy or too sad.

I pound on Mark's door until he yells, "Come in!"

"Can you turn this down?" I say, my voice extra loud to be heard over the noise.

Mark is sitting on his bed, which is a wreck, strumming his guitar. He's playing music on his iPhone through his amp, the amp that apparently isn't good enough anymore.

"What?" Mark says. He knows he can't hear me, but he won't touch the volume knob.

So I do. I turn it all the way down.

"Hey, what's wrong with you?" Mark sits up and reaches for the volume. "You don't come into a man's room, messin' with stuff."

"I can barely hear myself think!" I say angrily. "Other people live here, and you're torturing us with the noise!"

I don't know why I'm so upset, but it's just not my day.

"Whatever, Zoe," Mark says. "You walk around bothering everybody about this cookie dough thing."

"I do not!"

"Yes, you do," Mark says calmly. "You're not the only one with goals, Zoe."

"Well, I need that laptop for my *future*," I say. "You want an amp for what? So you can play louder?"

Mark stops strumming his guitar and looks at me.

"Are you serious?" he asks.

"What?"

"You think I play just to be loud?"

"And because you think it's cool?"

"Zoe, you ever think that maybe music means as much to me as writing means to you?"

I don't answer.

"Exactly," Mark says. "You only think about yourself."

"But the WordPro—"

"Is no more important than my guitar, or me going to Berklee."

"What's Berklee?" I wrinkle my nose.

"Berklee College of Music," Mark says. "Look it up."

"I would, if we had a decent computer," I say snarkily.

"Ha ha," Mark says. "Well, I guess you should exit my room and go sell some dough, then."

"Maybe I will."

"Here's some motivation," Mark says, turning his music up super-loud.

"Stop! Go to the Berklee place already!" I say. Mark laughs and does this whiny thing on his guitar that doesn't sound half-bad. I make a mental note to research Berklee the next time I'm in the computer lab at school.

Instead of going downstairs, I head to my room and dump all my fundraiser stuff on my bed. All the lines on my order form are filled, and I only have four spaces left on the one Felix gave me.

"I'm gonna need another one of these," I say to myself.

A few nights ago I called my grandparents and my aunt Sharon for orders. There've gotta be more people I can call today. I grab the house phone and call Mom at work.

"Hello?"

"Hi, Mom, it's Zoe. What's Uncle Larry's number?"

"Zoe? Sweetie, I'm kinda busy at the moment," Mom says. I can hear voices and movement in the background.

"Can you text it to Mark?" I ask. I don't add that if I had a phone, she could just text the number to me.

"We'll see," Mom says. "Check the kitchen drawer for my address book, okay? I'll call you guys later."

Click.

Okay, then.

I tear apart the kitchen junk drawer until I find Mom's old-school flower address book. Uncle Larry's number is in there, so I decide to call him first. He's Mom's only brother, and I hope he likes cookies.

No answer. I leave him a message, all bubbly and excited, and make sure to say the website for online orders twice.

I dial a number for Aunt Mabel and Uncle Coleman, who I really don't remember, but I think they live somewhere in Georgia. When Uncle Coleman answers, I make sure to say I'm Zoe, Lenette Sparks's daughter.

"Hold on, now, lemme get Mabel," he says in a Southern drawl that reminds me of Mr. Logan. My aunt Mabel is super-hyped when she comes to the phone.

"Zoe? How you doin', baby?" she says, the smile oozing from her voice.

"I'm doing great," I say. I tell her about school and Mark and Mom. I don't mention Daddy's layoff.

"Well, my school is doing a cookie dough fundraiser, and I'm calling my family members to see if they're able to help support me."

It takes a while to explain to Aunt Mabel that she can order online and the cookie dough will be shipped to her.

"Oh, I'll have to get Maxine to help me with all that," Aunt Mabel says. "That's my granddaughter. If it's electronic, she knows how to work it. I'll get a pen to write down the *www* address."

After a few more minutes of repeating the information, we hang up, but not before Aunt Mabel tells me to not be a stranger and to call more often.

I keep flipping through Mom's address book and call random family members. When the lady who answers Cousin Lou's phone number tells me he died last year, I decide it's time to stop.

I write down the orders I got, crossing my fingers that

people remember to place their orders and pay online. I call Felix to tell him how intense it was to call people I really didn't know. He doesn't answer, though, so I eat a cup of yogurt and go upstairs to make a deal with Mark. I'll use my own money to order a pizza for lunch if he uses his fancy headphones for the rest of the day!

Chapter 12

Snowflower

"**Okay, Zoe, I think** you've crossed the line on this cookie dough sale," Mom says, putting her cell phone on the counter.

I'm spending the morning with her at Snowflower, which is usually fun. But the look on her face right now? Not fun.

"Huh?" I ask innocently from the table where I've been cutting red ribbon.

"That was my cousin Gerald," she says. "He said you called and left him a message?"

"Ummm . . ."

"Zoe." Mom looks serious. "Please tell me you didn't go through my book and call every number you saw."

"No, Mom," I say. *I only called the ones in the "family" section.*

101

"Zoe, this is the second phone call I've received."

"Did Uncle Larry call?"

"No, he did not," Mom says, irritation creeping into her voice. "But my aunt Mabel did. She was happy to hear from you, but also surprised. You can't call people out the blue."

"Why not?" I ask. "They're family."

Mom sighs.

"Numbers might be changed, people might be . . ." Her voice trails off.

"Not alive?" I say.

Mom stares at me.

"You didn't."

"Yep," I say. "Called Cousin Lou. I did *not* get an order on that one."

Mom's mouth drops open a little. Then she busts up laughing, which I'm definitely not expecting.

"Zoe, you're something else," she says, shaking her head.

"What's with the giggles?" Mom's boss, Miss Pat, comes from the back of the shop with a tub of red roses. She's kinda old, kinda not, and you'll never see her sitting down. Me and her get along great.

"My daughter," Mom says, shaking her head. "She's on a mission to sell, what, Zoe, three hundred tubs of cookie dough?"

"Noooo, Mom," I groan. I turn to Miss Pat. "I need to be the top seller in my school so I can win a Horizon WordPro. You've heard me talk about that laptop, right, Miss Pat?"

"Only a million times," Miss Pat says.

"A million times, and no one has bought it for me yet," I say, eyeing Mom. "So I'm taking matters into my own hands to get it. Simple!"

"Oh, you're far beyond simple, missy," Mom says. She tells Miss Pat about some of my selling tactics. Miss Pat howls when Mom gets to the part about calling Cousin Lou, may he rest in peace.

"See, I knew there was a reason I liked you," she says, pointing the stem of a rose at me. She's separating them into bunches of twelve. "A go-getter; a girl with some spunk!"

"Exactly!" I say.

"How many orders do you have?" Miss Pat asks.

I give her my number and also tell her about Amaya. Miss Pat frowns.

"Oh, naw, we can't have Amaya Shaw snatching this from you. Put me down for five tubs; grandkids comin' up for spring break next month. You take cash?"

I spread my catalog and order forms on the counter, and Miss Pat writes down her order. By then it's about time for the shop to open.

"We gonna be slammed the next few days, with Valentine's this week," Miss Pat says. "Tell you what, if you come and help us out, I'll let you have a little corner of the store to sell your cookie dough, all right?"

"For real?" I ask.

"Of course, for real!" Miss Pat laughs. "Entrepreneur to entrepreneur."

"Don't encourage the madness," Mom says.

"Oh, stop," Miss Pat says. "This girl has drive. I'd be a fool not to encourage it."

That makes me feel good—better than I have since, well, since the fundraiser started.

"I can come right after school," I say.

"And I hope you have no Sunday plans, because we'll definitely need you tomorrow."

"No problem," I say. I'll have to spruce up my signs, maybe add glitter and stickers so they pop. Miss Pat interrupts my thoughts by handing me a broom.

"No time like the present, right, miss lady?"

"Right," I say. I get to work on the stems, leaves, and dirt that always find their way onto the floor at Snowflower. I realize really quickly that it doesn't matter how much I sweep; everything will be back down there in an hour.

Sidebar, do you know how much money is spent just on flowers for Valentine's Day? A ton! I'm writing an article about it for journalism, so I've researched the numbers. Still, I'm actually surprised by how busy it gets, with people dropping by or calling in their V-Day orders. Being at Snowflower gives me the perfect insider view for "The business side of love," and I take notes in my idea notebook every spare second I get. Should be a pretty provocative piece for Miss Douglas.

"Twelve dozen roses, Pat," Mom says, hanging up the phone after an order.

"He either loves her or he's in trouble," Miss Pat says, and she and Mom crack up.

Daddy comes by around one to bring Mom lunch and pick me up.

"Enjoy your day," Miss Pat says. "There will be no handsome daddy to pick you up tomorrow."

"Ahhhh, see, Zoe? Your dad still has it!" Daddy grins and nudges me. I don't point out that it's an *old lady* who just called him handsome.

"Don't get the big head, now." Miss Pat gives Daddy a hug. She thinks she's whispering, but I hear her tell him, "It's gonna be all right; you hang in there."

"You're going again tomorrow?" Daddy asks me in the car. I tell him about my deal with Miss Pat, and his face gets super-serious. Oh boy. I feel some shade coming.

But it doesn't.

"You know what, Zoe? I love your determination," Daddy says. "You've always had that. Like *no* means nothing to you."

"Does that mean you're sorry for all the times you put me on restriction?" I ask, giving Daddy the megawatt.

"Baby, I'm sorry! I'm not sorry!" Daddy starts singing that old song and I cringe.

"Okay, okay, I get it!" I try to cover his mouth. "Please stop!"

We get home in one piece, though my ears hurt almost as bad as when I come from a practice with the CRIM. I grab the home phone to call Felix, but he doesn't answer . . . again! I leave him a message asking if he can come by Snowflower tomorrow and help with the sale.

He doesn't call me back.

Chapter 13

When the Sugar Hits the Fan

Miss Pat wasn't lying about how busy it would be today. I'm exhausted by eleven, and we've only been open for a couple of hours! It's like they saved up a million tasks, just for me.

"I sure do wish you could drive, Miss Zoe," Miss Pat says. "I'd have you delivering, too!"

Instead of me, though, Miss Pat has hired two drivers to work for the week. And yes, I sell both of them tubs of cookie dough a few minutes after meeting them.

"Mom, can I just miss school on Tuesday so I can help you guys?" I ask after I make another sale.

Mom gives me the Buttons Face and I instantly regret asking.

"Zoe, you have lost your mind if you think I'm gonna pull you from school to sell cookie dough." She hands me a damp cloth. "Why don't you wipe these counters down."

I sigh and drag the cold cloth across the counters, then grab the broom and sweep up again. Third time so far.

Snowflower sells more than just flowers; Miss Pat has vases, wind chimes, greeting cards, and other little trinket gifts that people like to buy when there's a holiday. Whenever someone walks close to where my cookie dough table is set up, I stop what I'm doing and race over with a smile and my sales pitch. I think some of my sales come from people thinking I'm a Girl Scout, but hey, I'm not complaining.

Miss Pat orders a pizza and pop for lunch, and we gobble down slices before things pick up again. She calls it the "folks gettin' out of church" rush, and she isn't lying! I'm glad business is good for her, but I just don't get it. Are flowers that big of a deal? I'd rather have cookie dough.

"You going too far now," Miss Pat tells me after I say that to one of her customers.

"Don't complain," Mom says with a laugh. "I told you she was something else!"

I'm pretty much wilted by three-thirty, and Mom suggests I go down to Mango Bay to see if Felix is there.

"Don't worry, I'll handle your sales," she says. "You look like you need an *oooh-weee* smoothie."

I think I perk up just at the mention of the smoothie.

At the restaurant, Felix's dad makes THE best smoothies in the world. The amazing thing is, they're always different each time, because he doesn't follow a set recipe. Everyone calls them the "*oooh-weee* smoothie" because that's pretty much what you say after one sip.

Mom hands me some money and sends me into the cold. The puffy, wet snowflakes are pretty but no good for my hair, so I pull my hood over my head tight and walk fast. Mango Bay is only a few businesses down from Snowflower, but my face feels icy when I open the door and get hit with the familiar smells and sounds of the restaurant. Reggae music plays from the speakers, and the only two people inside chair-dance to the beat in their booth.

I don't see Felix around, which is strange since it's a weekend. But what's even weirder is that I don't see Mr. or Mrs. Fields, either. Usually at least one of them is around to greet customers. The guy wiping down tables looks up and smiles at me. I think he's a cousin or something.

"Hey, friend of Felix, am I right?" he asks.

"Yep," I say. "I'm Zoe. Is he here?"

"Nah, the superstar isn't here today," the guy says.

"What about Mr. and Mrs. Fields?" I ask.

"They will probably be in a little later," he says. "Can I get you something?"

"Ummm, do you know how to make the *oooh-weee* smoothies?" I ask.

The guy laughs.

"Do I know how?" he asks, his voice getting animated. "Who you think taught Delbert?"

He goes to the kitchen, and I sit at one of the front tables, wondering where in the world the Fields family is. I don't think I've ever been in Mango Bay without one of them around. They call the restaurant their firstborn child and say that Felix is actually second.

I hear the blender going in the kitchen, and a few minutes later the guy comes back with two smoothies. I pay him, throw my hood over my head, and power walk back to Snowflower.

"Nobody was there," I say, handing Mom her smoothie and taking a sip of mine.

Okay, pause. You know *oooh-weee* smoothies are beyond good if we would buy them in the middle of winter. But what I'm sipping right now is *not* an *oooh-weee* smoothie. The fruit isn't blended to perfection, and chunks keep clogging my straw. The flavor isn't right, either. It's an *oooh-noooo!* smoothie.

"What do you mean, nobody was there?" asks Mom. She tilts her head to the side a tiny bit after her first taste of the smoothie.

"Felix or his parents," I tell her. I set the smoothie down on the counter. Disappointing.

"That's odd. Maybe he had a meet?" Mom says, but then the phone rings and she's back to being busy.

I smack my hand to my head. Duh! It's Sunday, which means it's Felix's championship meet, the one I told him I'd go to. I try to rewind my brain; maybe I didn't say I would *definitely* go. But I know for sure I left a message on his phone asking him to come to Snowflower today to help me sell. So he knows I forgot. That's why he hasn't been answering his phone.

"You okay, Zoe?" Mom asks. Her gaze drifts over to my table, where two ladies are reading my sign.

"Yeah," I say. I walk over and half-heartedly give my sales pitch. They don't order anything. I take down my signs and pack up my things.

"Can I call Daddy to pick me up?" I ask Mom. "I don't feel good."

Mom gets the Shadow Face for a second and puts her hand on my forehead. Typical Mom thing to do, but I'm pretty sure there's no fever.

"Hold on a second," she says, disappearing into the office area. She comes back with both our coats. I grab my bag and say goodbye to Miss Pat, and we head to the car.

I sit inside and turn up the heat while Mom brushes the snow off the car. I check the time on the dashboard: 4:48. Too late to try and go to Felix's meet. I feel awful.

"All right, what's up, Zoe?" Mom asks. "I know something's wrong if you stop slinging cookie dough all on your own."

"I missed Felix's championship meet," I tell her. "He's gonna hate me."

Mom sighs.

"Ahhh, so that's why no one was at the restaurant," she says. "Did you tell him you were gonna go?"

"Yeah," I say. "Kinda, I guess."

"He's not gonna hate you," Mom says, rubbing my arm. "But I'm sure he's disappointed. This whole fundraiser has really consumed you."

"What's wrong with that?" I ask. "Why can't everyone just let me focus on this for three weeks and, you know, understand that I'm busy?"

Mom thinks for a second.

"You mean, why can't your family and friends understand that you're gonna be busy and unavailable for three weeks? That they should just be on pause?"

"Mo-om, that's not what I meant," I groan. It sounds bad when she says it like that.

"It's not?" Mom asks. I stare at my boots. "Listen, sweetie, everyone wants you to reach your goal, but is it worth it if you have to neglect other relationships or responsibilities?"

This is probably a rhetorical question, but my answer is a strong *maybe*. Mom continues before I can say it.

"What if Daddy was only focused on getting a new job right now, and he ignored the rest of us until he got one?" Mom asks. "Or if he didn't take the trash out or drive you to school or make lasagna until he met his goal?"

I lean my head against the cold window, stuck between agreeing with Mom and not. When we get home, she parks and comes inside with me.

"You're not going back?" I ask.

"Nope, I told Miss Pat this was important. I'll go in early tomorrow."

Great. Now I feel even worse. Mom left work early to be with me, and I couldn't even forget my sales for one day to watch Felix swim. Mom watches my face closely.

"It's gonna be okay, Zo Zo," she says. "Give him a call and apologize. See how you can make it up to him."

I grab the phone and call Felix. Straight to voice mail.

"I'm gonna go to my room," I tell Mom. She gives me a big hug.

"Okay, sweetie. Chili and cornbread for dinner."

"Cool."

I flop onto my bed and check for messages from Felix. Nothing. I hate to admit it, but I wouldn't even mind seeing one of his #upgrade messages. I type a message to him and then stare at it for a few seconds. Maybe it would be better if I just talked to him in person. First thing tomorrow. I erase the message and toss my phone onto my pillow.

When I turn over, I see my Horizon WordPro pictures on the wall. I remember my mission. It's not like I'm choosing the WordPro over Felix. It's my best friend, and the best machine.

"You got this, Zoe," I tell myself. I only have until Friday to sell, and after that, everything will be normal again. There's no way I can lose to Amaya, especially with Felix mad at me. I have to show him it was all worth it.

I open my backpack and study my order forms. Sixty-seven orders, and five days to go. I open the pencil case and start counting the money. I grab my calculator and add up all the orders. Then I count the money again. Then again.

Something isn't right.

I count one last time and drop the calculator to the floor. Just when I thought the day couldn't get any worse, it just did.

I'm $213 short.

Chapter 14

The Irony of Victory

I get to Mr. Boyd's room right before the bell rings, which kills my plan to talk to Felix before school. I smile and wave to him as I slide into my chair, but he just gives a small nod and looks down at his desk. Not a good sign.

"All right, guys, this is the last count we'll do before our cookie dough fundraiser is over. Let's get some good numbers on the board!"

He's basically giddy with excitement when he gets to Amaya.

"Sixty-three sales," Amaya says proudly.

This should be a moment when I'm beyond hyped, because I have more sales than Amaya, and she probably hit up everybody at her dad's job. But without the missing money, my sales don't even matter. For once, I don't have any genius ideas to fix this.

"Zoe? You with us this morning?" Mr. Boyd calls my name for what must be the second time. Amaya snickers behind me.

"Sixty-seven," I say with a sigh.

Mr. Boyd chuckles.

"I guess this is getting boring for you now, huh?" he says. He writes my number, somebody other than Felix yells our total, and then the morning announcements come on. I barely pay attention until the end.

"A big congratulations to Kentwood's very own Felix Fields, who took first place in the State Championship swim meet yesterday. Felix placed first in the fifty-yard freestyle and fifty-yard relay!"

Our class claps for Felix. When I turn around, he's grinning. Until he sees me. Then the smile slips from his face so fast.

"Congratulations," I tell him as we head down the hall.

"Thanks," Felix says without looking over.

"Felix, I'm sooo sorry about the meet," I say.

"It's all good," he says. "Hey, I guess I should congratulate you, too. You got more sales than Amaya."

"Well, not exactly," I say. I can't tell if he's being sarcastic or not, but I've been dying to tell someone about the missing money.

"You will not believe what happened! I was counting the money—"

I stop talking abruptly for two reasons: (1) Amaya walks up beside us, and she's the last person who needs to know about my dilemma. (2) Because of the look Felix is giving me. It's like he's totally and completely annoyed.

I mean-mug Amaya, ready for the drama I know she's about to bring. She glares at me for a second, then flashes Felix a smile.

"Congrats again, Felix," she says. "The meet was fun; I didn't know swimming could be so exciting!"

"Thanks!" Felix actually *smiles*! "I been trying to tell y'all!"

I know I shouldn't say anything, but I can't stop myself.

"Wait. You went?"

"Yeah," Amaya says. "It was the *championship*."

Ouch. I can't think of anything to say. I don't have to, though, because Amaya has plenty.

"My dad thought you were super-fast; did I tell you he swam in high school and college?" Amaya's talking a mile a minute, and she somehow finds a way to walk in between Felix and me.

"Anyway, he's gonna take me to a college meet, if you wanna come?"

"That would be tight," Felix says.

I slow down as those two keep walking. Neither one even notices I'm gone.

Chapter 15

Will You Be My Millionaire?

I hate cookie dough.

And fundraisers and layoffs and swimming and big brothers who make noise. Most of all, I hate when my Zoe Mode isn't working. Like now.

I'm up way before my alarm because I couldn't sleep all night. The ride with Felix after school yesterday was beyond awkward. I got dropped right at Snowflower, and Felix didn't ask if I could come by Mango Bay. Not that I expected him to. And when Mrs. Fields said, "Come by later for something sweet!" I took one look at Felix's face and told her we'd be really busy at the shop. She sent a sweet bun with Felix anyway, and he looked like it was torture to hand it to me.

I also stayed up all night trying to figure out what

happened to $213. I mean, I know I didn't spend it, and I've had that money with me everywhere! Could someone have taken it? Would Amaya be that mean? Why was she at Felix's meet anyway?

The questions don't stop coming, and I keep returning to the same thing: What am I going to do? Beyond standing on the side of the road with a sign, there's no way I can replace the money. Since Daddy has no job, there's no way I can ask my parents, either. I can only imagine the Shadow Face Mom would have. Permanently.

I give up on sleep and decide I have nothing to lose.

"This is for you," I whisper to my WordPro posters after I turn on my lamp. I dig around in my closet until I find the wig I wore last Halloween when I dressed up like Beyoncé. Next I dig around under my bed for the corny sunglasses I got at the fair. I grab a hat to top it off and put everything in my bag. I put the pencil case with all the rest of the money at the top of my closet.

I flip over one of my signs and write a completely different message in huge letters. *FUND THE FUTURE! SUPPORT KENTWOOD ACADEMY!* By the time I'm done, my alarm clock is beeping. Since I know I'll need them later, I put on thermals under my clothes, even though I'll be itchy all day. I'm not 100 percent sure of this plan, and I really wanna call Felix to see what he thinks.

But since I can't, I wash up, walk downstairs, and eat every heart-shaped pancake Mom puts on my plate.

"Either my pancakes are good, or you're starving," Mom says, watching me stuff my mouth.

"Both," I say. Something about being up all night made my stomach work overtime.

"Happy Valentine's Day, Zo Zo," Daddy says, sliding a red envelope across the table toward me.

"Thanks, Daddy," I say, feeling instantly worse that I didn't get anything for either of them. Was I supposed to?

"And because I like to make it rain . . ." Daddy wiggles his eyebrows and showers me and Mom with candy hearts. Mom laughs and I groan.

"Daddy, stop!" I say. Candy hearts land in my plate and in my signature hair puff.

"What? You can't stand the rain?" Daddy asks. Mom laughs like he's the funniest thing ever, which leads to a gross smooch.

"Hey, I gotta get to school, you guys!" I remind them. Luckily they break it up quick.

"All right, madam, your chariot awaits," Daddy says. Then he winks at Mom. "I'll be returning for you, sweet lady."

I race to the car before I throw up.

Mark took Mom's car today because he has some gig

after school. That means Daddy is our designated Uber. He seems to be okay with it, though.

"You all right, Sales Queen?" he asks me once we turn onto the main street.

I almost tell him everything right then. But I have this one last plan to try, and if it works, no one will have to know about the mess I'm in.

"Yes, I'm fine," I say.

"Hmm." Daddy studies me. "I don't have to worry about some boy giving you chocolates or anything else today, do I?"

I cover my face with my hand.

"Do I need to talk to Felix?"

"Daddy!" Talking to Felix is definitely not an option.

"I'm just playing, Zoe," he says, and his face gets serious for a second. "You sure everything's okay? You seem a little off."

Again I clamp my mouth shut so I don't tell him just how off I am. Two hundred and thirteen dollars off. I tell Daddy I'm worried about a math test we have first thing, and he starts reciting his times tables. I don't bother stopping him.

I get to school on time and spend most of the day burning hot because of the thermals as I watch kids give their friends silly Valentine's Day stuff. Even Miss Douglas gets into it and has heart cookies for us. We wrote love-themed articles last week, and she lets us know which ones will be in the *Buzz* this week.

I'm both excited and nervous when the bell rings at the end of the day. I walk over to Felix near the doors where parents pick up.

"Hey, um, I have a ride today," I tell him. I don't know about him, but I'd rather not relive yesterday's drive together. It's technically not a full lie, since Daddy's been picking me up a lot more since the layoff. Still, Felix seems surprised when I say this and, I don't know, maybe a little disappointed, too.

"Okay, cool," he says. He lifts his backpack higher on his shoulder and opens the door.

"See ya," he says once his minivan pulls into the line.

"Felix, wait," I say. But I'm speaking too softly and he's already gone. There's a gust of cold air that makes me shudder and rethink my plan. It's not too late to run to Felix's minivan and jump in. My feet don't move, though, and as soon as the Fieldses pull off, I head toward the baseball field.

Once I'm there, I hurry around to the side of the equipment shed and dig into my backpack. I put on the wig and sunglasses, which actually make my face a bit warmer. I had to fold up my sign to fit, but I smooth it out as best as I can. Next up, location, location, location.

I choose the corner of MLK Boulevard and Wall Street because it's pretty busy but far enough from school. I'm freezing by the time I get there, and I realize that I have no idea how I'll get home. There's no turning back now, so I take a deep breath, hold up my sign, and wait.

The minutes and cars roll by. Nobody stops. I hold the sign higher, bounce it around a little. Nothing. I get some strange looks, and I'm sure it's because of the wig and sunglasses. Also, I'm not that tall. And I have a backpack. Okay, okay, this is an awful idea. The reality hits me harder than the cold, and at the exact same time it does, I see a silver Subaru coming toward me. No way could that be . . .

I raise the sign to cover my face, and I hold my breath. A few seconds pass, and then a horn starts blaring. Oh. No.

"Zoe! ZOE!"

I slowly lower the sign. Mark has the passenger window down and is glaring at me from the driver's seat.

"Get in the car!" he yells. I do what he says without arguing. He goes in on me the moment I close the door.

"What the hell are you doing, Zoe?"

Whoa.

"Language, Mark Sparks," I say, just how Mom would. He doesn't find it funny.

"This ain't a game, Zoe! You trying to sell cookie dough on the *street*?"

"Technically, I wasn't selling cookie dough," I say in a small voice. "I was asking for donations."

Mark still looks utterly disgusted.

Zoe Mode, Zoe Mode, Zoe Mode, I tell myself. But it doesn't work. My eyes are already watering from the cold, so I don't bother trying to stop the monsoon that comes now. Mark's face goes from disgust and anger to concern. When I catch my breath, I spill my guts about the missing money and how I've looked everywhere for it.

"I can't turn in my orders with missing money!"

I picture Amaya's smug face and her manicured fingers wrapped around my WordPro, and more angry tears leak out.

"Did you tell Mom and Dad?" Mark asks.

"No," I say. "Daddy just lost his job, Mark. What's he gonna do? This will only make him more stressed."

And it makes me seem like a baby who can't do anything on her own.

"I get that," Mark says. "But this is kind of a big problem. Selling cookie dough, getting donations; whatever you were doing on the side of the road isn't gonna fix it."

I sigh. Of course, I *know* that. But I also have no other ideas. I turn to explain this to Mark, but then I notice that he has on black dress pants and shoes, and a red bow tie peeks over the top of his coat.

"Wait, why are you dressed like that?" I ask.

"Because I'm on my way to a gig," Mark says.

"Ummm, are you gonna drop me home first?"

"Nope," Mark says. "That'll make me late."

"Soooo . . ."

"Soooo, how were you gonna get home after your road-side routine?" Mark asks.

I sigh again.

"I didn't plan that part yet," I say.

"Yeah. You're riding with me," Mark says with finality. I guess it's what I deserve; dumb idea equals torture by the CRIM.

Mark drives for what seems like forever and finally pulls into a hotel parking lot.

"You guys are playing at a hotel?" I ask. Who would willingly ask for that? What about all the poor guests?

"Rodney's parents got us a gig playing at a Valentine's Day party," Mark says. He calls Mom to let her know I'm with him. Then he grabs his guitar and amp from the trunk, and I carry his bag of cords and guitar pedals.

"This looks pretty fancy," I say as we walk through the lobby and follow the red and white balloons and signs pointing us to one of the ballrooms. "You nervous?"

"No." Mark makes a face. "Why do you think we practice?"

Probably another rhetorical question, and I'm sure Mark doesn't want my answer. Truth is, what's the point of practice when you end up sounding the same? Anyway, I keep my comments to myself because I'm speechless when we walk into the ballroom.

"Whoa," I say. "This is a for-real party!"

It looks like a giant peppermint in here; all the tables have red or white tablecloths, and even the chairs have covers and bows on them. Everyone is wearing the same colors, and when someone yells, "Crimson and cream!" I grin.

"Oh, I get it! CRIMson!" I say.

"Uh, no," Mark says. "It's their frat and sorority colors. But that does make a lot of sense. Dang, we shoulda picked up on that! We coulda made signs!"

"See? Writers notice important details like that," I tell him.

"Whatever," Mark says. "And take off that wig, Zoe."

"Oh, sorry!" I say. I took off the shades in the car but forgot all about the wig. I pull it off and stick it in Mark's bag. I spruce up my puff and follow Mark to where Chad is setting up his drums. Rodney's there, too, already messing around on the keyboard. No sign of Beanie yet.

"It's Roadie Zoe!" Rodney says, reaching over to mess up my puff. I move my head just in time.

"Singing with us tonight?" Chad asks.

"Yeah, maybe I'll replace Beanie," I joke.

"Not today, you won't!"

Beanie comes up behind me, and I can't move my head fast enough to keep him from my hair. What is it about my puff that they can't resist?

"Quit it!" I scold. Beanie just laughs and fist-bumps the other guys.

Rodney's parents come over and ask the band if they need anything. I bite my tongue to keep from saying they need muted mics and a soundproof room.

"And, Miss Zoe, are you sitting with these guys, or do you want to be at a table?" asks Rodney's mom. To me, she looks like a model. All. The. Time. #Goals.

"She'll be with the band," Mark says before I can open my mouth.

"Okay, well, you're welcome to the food if you want," Rodney's mom says. "Do you like filet mignon?"

"Uhhh." My face twists up before I can stop it. Rodney's mom chuckles.

"No worries, I really don't, either," she says secretively. "I'll make sure they bring you some mac and cheese."

Rodney's dad—who also looks like a model; I don't know what happened with Rodney, but he does *not* look like them—comes over and tells the guys they can start playing.

"Here's the list of songs we talked about. Make sure to play those two first," he says, pointing to the piece of paper. He checks to make sure his wife is off mingling with other people. "Y'all better not mess this up, understand?"

I swallow hard. Has Rodney's dad never heard the

CRIM before? They're pretty much guaranteed to mess something up.

"Dad, chill," Rodney says. "We got this."

"Yeah, make it happen," his dad says before joining his wife.

"No pressure," I say, patting Rodney on the arm.

"Girl, please," Rodney says. "Get out your little pen and paper and take notes."

"Here's your chair," Mark adds, patting a seat off to the side. "Sit down and don't move."

"I'm not five years old, you know," I tell him.

"Riiiight," Mark says.

He and the guys put their fists together and say something corny, and then Chad counts it off and the music starts.

Wait. Actual music? Okay, I'm beyond shocked. They're playing a song I recognize, and the people there get all excited. Some guy comes to the main podium and welcomes everybody, and then the CRIM starts playing their own music. It's not bad, surprisingly. Rodney's parents must've told them to tone it down, because it's way more jazzy than cringey. I study the people at the fancy tables. Even though they're eating, a lot of them are bobbing their heads and grooving to the music. Some people even get on the dance floor and get busy. Maybe what Rodney said isn't a bad idea. I grab my idea notebook and an orange pen.

I write about how hard work and dedication pay off. If it works for this band, it'll work for anyone. Even me.

On the ride home, I tell Mark the truth.

"You guys were pretty good," I say.

"*Pretty* good?" Mark makes a face.

"Okay, okay," I admit. "It was borderline amazing. I was not embarrassed to be related to you."

"Wowwwww," Mark says. "And how do you think I felt seeing my sister on the side of the road looking like a broke-down Beyoncé?"

"Can we maybe stop bringing that up?" I ask. "Like, forever?"

"Nah, that was a pretty unforgettable sight," Mark says.

Great. He's probably gonna run his mouth about this to Mom and Daddy, which means permanent restriction. And I wouldn't mind that at all if I had the WordPro. But my situation right now is looking a lot like no WordPro, no Felix, and no nothing.

"Relax, Zo Zo," Mark says. "Like you said, telling Mom and Dad will only stress them out. They have enough to worry about, and so do you. Just promise me you won't do no stupid stuff like that again."

"I won't," I say.

"Let's just say you owe me," Mark says. And although he's grinning, I'm not really sure that happiness is up next for me.

Chapter 16

The SuperMark

I thought I was done crying. Guess not.

When I wake up, there's a guitar-pick box on my desk, only when I open the box, there are no guitar picks inside.

Two hundred and thirteen dollars are inside, along with a note.

> THIS IS A LOAN, ZO ZO . . . I KNOW WHERE
> YOU LIVE! IF YOU DON'T END UP TOP SELLER, THE
> INTEREST RATE IS 50%, SO MAKE SURE YOU WIN
> THAT STUPID LAPTOP.
>
> ~MARK

I read his note a couple of times, and I can't believe my brother would be this nice. I mean, he's been saving for a while now for his music stuff; he doesn't spend money on anything. This has to be a joke. I count the bills again. Wow. Who knew I had the best big brother in the world?

When I put the money with the rest of my stash, I can't help thinking about this whole fundraiser thing and how I pretty much went after it and ignored everyone else, including Mark, my parents, and especially Felix. Ugh! I should've paid attention and gone to his big meet. I open my notebook, and this time the ideas I get have nothing to do with cookie dough and everything to do with trying to make things right. First up is Felix.

I beg Daddy to stop by the store on the way to school (not Palace Farms, of course).

"Why didn't you do this last night when you were with Mark?" Daddy asks as I scan the millions of choices in the card aisle.

"I didn't have the idea last night," I tell him. I pick up a card, read it, put it back.

"What are you looking for, exactly?" Daddy asks.

"The perfect card," I say. Three cards later, and I'm not having much luck.

"We're gonna have to go, or you'll be late for school," Daddy tells me, checking his watch.

"Okay, okay, I'll hurry," I say. I spot a blue card with a teddy bear on the front. The second I open it I know it's the one.

The good thing about shopping a day after Valentine's Day is that all the candy is super-cheap. I grab a pack of mini candy bars (for me), then race to the frozen aisle for a box of ice cream sandwiches.

"Zoe, you realize those are going to melt, right?" Daddy says, raising an eyebrow. I stare at the box. Yeah, they probably will be a little melty. But I have to try this.

"Just trust me, Daddy," I say, pulling him to the self-checkout. "It's gonna be fine." *I hope.*

I get to school late; a real shocker. What's new this time is that Daddy parks the car and comes inside to sign me in.

Ms. Hamilton is sipping her coffee like usual, and while she's clearly not happy that I'm late again, she doesn't snap at me.

"Good morning, are you signing Zoe in?" Ms. Hamilton asks Daddy. Daddy flashes a smile. Wait, is that a megawatt? Wonder where he got that from.

"Yes, ma'am," Daddy says. "I had an errand that took longer than expected."

"Just sign here, and I'll write her a pass to first hour." Ms. Hamilton pushes a button and makes an announcement about a menu change for lunch. Interesting. I get another idea after watching her.

"Going to Mr. Boyd, right?" Ms. Hamilton asks. "Zoe?"

"Huh? Oh, yes. Mr. Boyd."

I take it as a sign when the phone rings and Ms. Hamilton stops writing my pass to answer. Out of the corner of my eye, I see Daddy put his pen down. It's now or never.

I lunge over the counter and push the intercom button.

"Attention, all students, Felix Fields is the best swimmer in the universe!"

"Zoe!" I feel Daddy tugging me, and Ms. Hamilton has a horrified expression on her face, but I'm not done yet.

"And he's also the best friend in the universe!" I yell before Daddy snatches me off the counter.

"What are you doing?" he says, looking both confused and upset. Ms. Hamilton finishes her phone call and immediately goes in on me.

"Zoe, absolutely not! You know the rules! Students cannot use the intercom system unless authorized by a school official."

"I'm sorry, Ms. Hamilton," I say. "I needed to do that. For a friend."

"It's not about what you think you needed to do," Daddy says sternly. "Your school has rules for a reason."

"I'm sorry," I say again. A few seconds pass, and I wait for either Daddy or Ms. Hamilton to say something. They glance at each other like they're not sure what to say. Finally Ms. Hamilton gives a big sigh.

"We'll take it from here, Mr. Sparks," she says. "Thank you for signing her in."

Daddy nods and turns to me.

"Zoe, behave yourself, understand? We'll talk more at home."

"Okay, Daddy. Have a magnificent day," I tell him. Daddy shakes his head and gives me a kiss on the forehead.

"You are something else," he says under his breath.

Ms. Hamilton hands me my pass, and I leave superquick, before she comes up with a punishment for school-intercom takeover.

Everyone stares at me when I walk into Mr. Boyd's class, including Felix. I'm guessing they all heard the announcement. I walk past my seat and plop the card and box of ice cream sandwiches on Felix's desk.

"You might wanna hurry on those," I tell him, nodding at the box. "Melting."

"Awwww," Amaya says annoyingly.

"Zoe, take your seat, please," Mr. Boyd says. "And what is that?"

Mr. Boyd peers at Felix's desk. Felix is already opening the box.

"Not in here, Mr. Fields," Mr. Boyd says. "Perhaps the kitchen crew will be nice enough to allow you to store that in the freezer."

Mr. Boyd writes Felix a pass to the cafeteria and con-tinues with his lesson. If I know Felix, half of those sand-wiches will be gone by the time he gets to the lunchroom, and hopefully his anger will be melting right along with them. If the sandwiches don't get him, the card has to. I tap my pencil nervously as I wait for him to return to class. I can't help smiling when he does, because I can see a small swipe of ice cream on his top lip. I try to catch his eye as he walks to his seat, but he doesn't look my way.

I go all day wondering if he's still mad, and I can't bring myself to ask him. I don't see him in the cafeteria at lunch, and he doesn't say anything to me until seventh hour in Miss Douglas's class. He finally speaks when we end up at the same table to review a pollution article in today's newspaper.

"Hey," he says.

"Hey," I reply.

"Thanks for the apology card and stuff."

"You're welcome," I tell him. "Did Ms. Lerner let you put the ice cream sandwiches in the freezer?"

"What ice cream sandwiches?" Felix asks sneakily.

"You ate them all?"

"Nah," Felix laughs, "there's still some left. I started getting brain freeze after two."

We're both quiet for a second, and I'm about to start apologizing all over again when Felix breaks the silence.

"So how are sales going?" he asks.

"Who cares about sales?" I say. "I almost lost my best friend! Felix, I'm really sorry about everything. I've been too obsessed with this stupid cookie dough. You know what? I'm tired of this whole fundraiser thing. I'm done!"

Felix looks at me like I've lost my mind.

"Ummm, Zoe, nah. You can't give up like that." Felix lowers his voice and leans in closer. "Amaya came to my youth group last night, and she's up to seventy sales! You can't stop now!"

I feel a pang in my chest, and I can't tell if it's because Amaya and Felix are getting close or because she's passed me in sales.

"She goes to your youth group now?" I ask.

"I guess she was bored." Felix shrugs. "She's really not that bad when she's by herself, I guess. I think she's got a lot going on at home."

"Who doesn't?" I ask, thinking about Daddy's job situation. "That doesn't mean you get to be a jerk."

"I know, right?" Felix says with a grin that reminds me of my recent jerk days.

"Hey, I just apologized!" I protest. "And I'm saying that you're more important than all the cookie dough in the universe."

"True," Felix says. "But don't use me as the reason why you lose."

Zoe Sparks, lose? Those words don't even go together! But I don't want to mess up with Felix again. Maybe there's a way to tame my Zoe Mode. . . .

"Your eyes are doing that twitching thing," Felix says. "So you have a plan yet?"

"Not quite," I admit.

"Perfect," Felix says.

He looks like he's gonna say something else, but Miss Douglas tells us it's time to switch partners and review our second article. Amaya works with Felix next, and that pang slides into my heart again. It stays there after school, when Felix immediately disappears into the crowd of students spilling outside. He doesn't even stop at his locker. I thought apologizing would fix things. Guess I'll move on with my list.

I have no homework when I get home, so I ask Daddy if he needs help making dinner. Mom said this will be her last late night at Snowflower, and Mark and the band are practicing for their next gig. I guess playing at the Valentine's banquet really helped them get popular.

"I'm just chillin' and grillin', so you're welcome to join me," Daddy says. We go back and forth from the toasty kitchen to the arctic patio to check on the burgers, which smell *amazing*. It feels good to only have to worry about buns, burgers, and rinsing lettuce.

"It's good to have normal Zo Zo tonight," Daddy says, draping one arm around my shoulder and flipping the burgers with his other hand.

"Dang, was I really that bad?" I ask. "I think you're being *dramatic*."

Daddy stops what he's doing, tilts his head, and goes all duck-lips on me.

"Sweetie, you tried selling cookie dough to the FedEx guy. You were reciting order numbers and cookie dough flavors in your sleep. Yes. You were that bad."

Yikes! He's probably right, because I do have every flavor and item number memorized.

The phone's ringing when we go inside, and when I pick it up, it's Felix.

"Listen, you gotta come to the restaurant with me after school tomorrow, okay?"

"For what?" I ask, sensing that he's in Felix-Is-a-Genius Mode.

"Just ask your parents if you can hang out. I have an idea."

"Felix, it's Wednesday. We have to turn in our sales on Friday," I say. Can't lie, though; now I'm wondering what he has planned.

"So? Just be there. I'm not gonna listen to you whine about how you coulda got that laptop."

"But didn't you say Amaya had—"

Felix cuts me off. "This ain't about Amaya. Stop with the excuses; I'm hanging up now."

And he does. I tried to fight it, but just like that, Zoe Mode is back.

Chapter 17

Money and Mangoes

"Okay, first you gotta promise me you won't be all obsessed like before," Felix says. We're riding in his mini-van to Mango Bay, and I'm already excited.

"Nobody wanna buy anything when you acting all desperate," Felix continues. I open my mouth to protest, but he just laughs. Mrs. Fields peers at us in the rearview mirror.

"Felix told you about the—"

"Mom!" Felix interrupts. "I haven't told her yet."

"Wait, your mom knows the idea?" I whisper. The suspense is really killing me now! Felix just grins and whistles like he didn't hear me. I say the first thing that comes to mind, the thing Daddy always says about me.

"You're something else, Fe Fe."

"Hey." Felix gets serious. "It's not too late to take you home."

He and I both know that's not gonna happen, and ten minutes later we're walking into the restaurant. Mr. Fields greets us with a grin.

"How ya like it?" he asks, holding up a yellow poster board with black-and-green lettering:

KENTWOOD NIGHT! ASK HOW TO GET 10% OFF YOUR BILL!

"What is—"

"Thanks, Dad, it's perfect," Felix says, cutting me off again. He pulls me to our special booth and finally tells me his idea.

"Check it out; from five p.m. to closing, my parents agreed to give people ten percent off their food if they order cookie dough from you," he tells me. "Pretty cool, right?"

Man, compared to me and my side-of-the-road idea, Felix is a genius for real!

"That's awesome! They really said yes to that?"

"How they gonna turn down a state champ?" Felix asks.

"Whatever." I grin.

We tape Mr. Fields's sign in the front window of the restaurant, then run outside to make sure we can see it okay. Inside the restaurant, Felix and I set up a small card table near the register. We cover it with a red tablecloth, and I arrange all my brochures and order forms.

"My dad said we can use this," Felix tells me, plopping a box on the table. When he opens it, I see four slots for dollar bills and a space for coins.

"It locks, too," he says. "I'll help you keep up with it."

We're all set when five o'clock hits. Not everyone asks what "Kentwood Night" means, but my ears always perk up when I hear somebody ask their server how they can save 10 percent. Then their heads turn toward our table, where I wave and give megawatt smiles. I think a part of me was expecting a stampede to hit our table. That does NOT happen. I do get fifteen orders, though, and Felix snaps a lot of good pictures for Mango Bay's social media accounts. By the end of the night, everyone's smiling. I keep thanking Mr. and Mrs. Fields for agreeing to their son's genius idea. I don't tell them, but I get a genius idea of my own to start a Community Buzz column in our paper. If Miss Douglas lets me, Mango Bay will be the first business I'll highlight.

"You're a real spunky girl, Miss Zoe," Mrs. Fields says, her accent sounding like a melody. "I always liked that."

"We're rootin' for you to have the most sales ever," Mr. Fields adds. He hands me a real *oooh-weee* smoothie with a wink. "You'll get another one of these when ya win."

Felix and I count up all my orders while we wait for Mom to come pick me up.

Eighty-two.

"Not bad," Felix says.

"You think it's enough?"

"I dunno. I guess we just gotta wait till tomorrow," says Felix.

Waiting. Something Zoe Sparks hates to do. I sip my *oooh-weee* smoothie and try to forget that in less than twelve hours, I will either be the owner of a brand-new Horizon WordPro . . .

Or not.

Chapter 18

And the Winner Is . . .

I wake up to Mom shaking my shoulder.

"Zoe, wake up, sweetie," she says. I pry my eyes open and groan. I feel like I got hit in the face with a volleyball. I tossed and turned most of the night, so I'm surprised I even fell asleep.

"We must've lost power in the night," Mom says. "Nobody's alarm went off, so you'll probably be a little late."

"Nooo!" I groan again. Why do I have the worst luck ever?

I get washed up and dressed in record time, then grab a bagel and apple on the way to the car. I can't help but sigh when I see the time inside the Jeep. I've missed the final sales tally. Right now there's a big, fat blank by my name, and it's killing me to not know what's beside Amaya's name. To make everything worse, Daddy can't come into the building to sign me in because he has an interview.

"I promise I'll call to excuse you, okay, sweetie?" he says.

"Don't forget, or I'll get another detention," I say. "And I'm not being dramatic, but that's not a good look for my record."

"Bye, Zoe." Daddy blows me a kiss and pulls off. I gear myself up to deal with Ms. Hamilton.

Dang, she frowns a little when she sees me, and she moves her chair to the side to block the intercom. I mean, c'mon, really? It's not like I'm gonna use the same move twice.

"Good morning!" I say cheerfully.

"Are we making tardiness a habit, Miss Sparks?" she asks.

"Not at all," I tell her. "We lost power this morning. My father will be calling to excuse me."

I can tell Ms. Hamilton doesn't believe me all the way, but she writes my pass and hands it to me without any fussing.

"Thanks," I tell her. "Have a great morning!"

"You too, dear," Ms. Hamilton says.

Wow, that's the nicest thing she's said to me. Like, ever. My hand is on the doorknob and I'm about to go into the hallway when the idea hits me. Let's just call it the final idea. I'm not sure what will happen, but my Zoe Mode says I have to try. I turn around.

"Ms. Hamilton?" I ask. She looks up from her desk at me.

"Yes?"

"Do you like cookies?"

"What?"

"Cookies," I say. "Do you like cookies? I mean, I know you like coffee, and donuts usually go with coffee, but I'm thinking maybe cookies do, too?"

Ms. Hamilton stares like she's trying to make sense of what I'm saying.

"Wait. No one has asked you to buy cookie dough for the fundraiser?" I ask her. I imagined that every kid in the school had already hit up every adult who works here, but maybe I was wrong.

"No," Ms. Hamilton says.

"All the kids at Kentwood, and no one has bothered to see if you, our dedicated attendance official, would like to order a tub of cookie dough?"

"Zoe, I think you should get to class," Ms. Hamilton says.

"I will, Ms. Hamilton," I tell her, pulling out the cookie dough brochure. "But it's the last day of the fundraiser, so technically, I'm your last chance to have one of these."

I open the brochure and pretty much plaster it in front

of her face. I hold my breath, hoping she doesn't shut me down. When I hear her say, "Hmm," I know I got her.

"I will do two jumbo tubs of oatmeal raisin," she tells me. "Do I write on here?"

"Yes, ma'am," I tell her. "And I can take cash or checks."

"You are something else, Zoe Sparks," Ms. Hamilton tells me. She hands me twenty-four dollars, which I add to my box of money. Daddy and I counted and recounted last night, and everything matched up perfectly.

As I walk down the hall to class, I realize that Ms. Hamilton and Daddy are right—I *am* something else. Something wonderful. Something brave. Something with eighty-four sales.

As usual, heads swivel when I walk into class. Amaya looks way too confident, and my heart starts to thump. What if she wins? I've never let my brain go there, because I *have* to have the WordPro! All these sales will be worthless if I don't win!

But then I see Felix, giving me the thumbs-up and being his normal chill self, and I start to feel a teeny bit better. I gave it my best shot. And if I don't win the Word-Pro today, I'll just have to activate Zoe Mode to figure out another way.

"Ah, we were all hoping you'd come walking through that door, Zoe," Mr. Boyd says with a smile. "We just finished our final count."

"Did our class win?" I ask.

"We won't know until next week," Mr. Boyd says, "when the school tallies the sales from all classrooms."

"Oh."

"Would you like to do the honor of writing your final number?" Mr. Boyd asks, handing me a Sharpie. "And you can turn in your order form and money as well."

I reach in my backpack and hand him both my order forms, plus the copy page Felix and I had to make at Mango Bay. I also give him the whole money box.

"This might be easier," I tell him. "Just make sure you return it to Felix when you're done."

I take the Sharpie from him and feel the spotlight on me as I walk to the poster board. I slowly scan from top to bottom, my heart racing fast when I get to Amaya's name.

My heart stops. I stare at her number. And then I write mine.

Amaya. 77

Zoe. 84

"Whooo!" Felix says when I step away and the class sees my number. He announces the class total and then says, "You won, Zoe!"

"Not so fast, Felix," Mr. Boyd says. "Zoe, your sales number is incredible, and you're definitely the top seller for Team Boyd. But remember, the school will be tallying orders to determine the top seller overall. I'm told we'll have those results early next week."

I almost collapse as I walk to my seat. More waiting??

Felix can't believe me when I tell him who my final sale was.

"Yo, you are outta control!" he laughs. I laugh, too. And I get ready to wait the whole weekend to see if it was all worth it.

Chapter 19

And the Winner Is . . . Part Two

I heard that the PTA is responsible for tallying up all the sales. Well, I think we should sign a petition to make them learn to count faster! I mean, shouldn't basic addition skills be required to be a member of the PTA anyway? I offer to write an article on the subject, but Miss Douglas shoots it down in the nicest way possible.

"I can't believe this is taking so long!" I tell Felix. He smacks his hand on our table.

"Zoe, chill!" he says. "Turn off the beast mode."

"Sorry," I say. The weekend was *torture,* especially since we had no school on Monday! The only thing that helped was taking Felix to Sprinkles for all-you-can-eat ice cream, and it was cool to watch videos from his championship meet. But as soon as my head hit my pillow that night, the fundraiser count was all I could think about!

It's rare that I daydream in Miss Douglas's class, but today it's so hard to focus! She's telling us that she'll be submitting our articles to her TV station for Young Journalist Week and that we could be featured on the air. All cool stuff, but it's like she's speaking another language. Just when I'm about to ask for a pass to go to the office and check on things, the intercom crackles and Ms. Hamilton's voice comes on. I suck in my breath and dig my fingernails into Felix's arm.

"Ow!" He snatches it away. "You left marks!"

"Shhhh!" I say.

"Good afternoon, Kentwood! First of all, thank you to all those who participated in this year's Dough for Dough Fundraiser. It has been a huge success, and it is because of your dedication. And now, the moment you've been waiting for: the announcing of our top classroom seller and our top student seller. The classroom with the most sales is . . . Mr. Boyd's sixth-grade class! And with a record-breaking eighty-four tubs of cookie dough sold, this year's top seller is sixth grader Zoe Sparks!"

Felix whoops beside me, and the class claps, but I feel like I'm floating above it all. Did. I. Really. WIN?

Ms. Hamilton's announcement continues.

"Cookie dough orders will be here in three weeks, on March thirteenth. Small orders will be sent home with you, but those of you with larger orders will need a parent or guardian to come pick them up. Thank you all for a successful fundraiser!"

"Guess you a boss now, huh?" Felix asks, nudging me.

"I don't know," I tell him. "I think I'm in shock."

"That's a first." Felix snickers.

"Just so you know, a first grader sold eighty-three tubs, so you *barely* won," Amaya announces. When we all turn to stare at her, she shrugs. "My mom's in the PTA."

"Hater!" Brandon says, fake-coughing into his fist. Amaya glares at him.

"Congratulations, Zoe," Miss Douglas says. "That's a whole lot of cookie dough."

"Thanks," I say. "Just wait till you read the articles I'll write on my WordPro."

"Looking forward to it," she says. "Although it's not the machine you type on that makes you good. It's the machine up here." Miss Douglas taps the side of her head and winks.

After school, I grab my stuff and run down to the office.

"Is Principal Bledsoe in her office?" I ask Ms. Hamilton.

"She's probably wrapping up bus duty, if you want to wait a few minutes," she says. "And congratulations on being the top seller. That's amazing!"

"Thanks," I say. "Couldn't have done it without you."

Literally.

"Zoe's here to see you," Ms. Hamilton says when Principal Bledsoe bustles into the office with a not-so-happy-looking kid.

"Sure; one second, Zoe," Principal Bledsoe says. "Ms. Hamilton, would you give Trey's grandfather a call to come pick him up?"

"Of course," Ms. Hamilton says, searching for the number.

"Thanks," Principal Bledsoe says. "And we're going to do *much* better tomorrow, right, Trey?"

Trey mumbles, "Yeah," and Principal Bledsoe pats his shoulder.

"Okay, Zoe, come on in."

I follow her into her office, glad I'm not in trouble.

"What can I help you with?" Principal Bledsoe asks cheerfully. Man, I don't know how she can smile after dealing with bad kids all day.

"I won't take much time," I tell her. "Just here for my Horizon WordPro GT. Orange, to be exact."

"Pardon me?"

"For being the top seller in the fundraiser," I explain. "The drone looked amazing, but I gotta have the WordPro, you know?"

"Ah, yes," Principal Bledsoe chuckles. "Congratulations on an incredible job. Did you think we have the prizes in the office?"

"Ummm, yeah?"

"Well, I wish I could hand one to you right now, sweetie, but as you can see"—she spreads her arms wide—"no prizes here."

And then she drops the bomb and tells me prizes usually ship *four to six* weeks *after* the cookie dough company gets all the order forms and money! FOUR TO SIX WEEKS!!

"The PTA is in charge of all that," Principal Bledsoe says, checking her watch.

"Principal Bledsoe, that is completely unacceptable!" I say. "Can you give me the PTA president's phone number? There has to be a faster way!"

Principal Bledsoe pauses, like she can't believe what I asked. Then she starts laughing. Hard.

"You're something else, Miss Zoe," she says. "I will let you know the second we receive your prize. You have a great afternoon, young lady."

Sigh. Dismissed.

"Thank you, Principal Bledsoe, I'll check in with you tomorrow."

I don't say that if I have to, I'll check back *every* day until my fingers are flying across the keys of my brand-new WordPro. But something tells me Principal Bledsoe already knows I will.

Yes. I'm something else.

Chapter 20

Special Delivery

It's two weeks later, and I probably should've thought about the whole delivery part of this fundraiser. I mean, the people gotta get their cookies, but it's eighty-four tubs of dough going all over the city! When I see all the boxes with my name on them in the gym, my mouth drops open. This is gonna be a loooooong night!

"I guess this is the part you didn't think about, huh?"

I turn and see Amaya beside me. *Here we go.* I'm about to tell her, *Yeah, I did think about this moment; the moment when I beat you!* But then she sighs and says, "Me neither."

Huh? Amaya being halfway, semi . . . un-mean?

"My dad's gonna be pissed," she says. "He hates clutter in his car."

I follow her gaze and see a ton of boxes with her name on them, too.

"Isn't it all just going to his job?" I ask. I'm curious to know what else she did to get to seventy-seven sales, but since I don't know if she's really being nice, I keep quiet.

"Yeah, and neighbors," Amaya says. "At his place and my mom's."

"Oh."

Amaya doesn't say anything else, but she really doesn't have to. I guess she doesn't get everything she wants after all. Who knows? Maybe I'll get to know her a little better. *Maybe.* The way Felix talks, she might actually be an okay person.

Daddy comes into the gym at the same time as Amaya's dad, and they couldn't be more different. First of all, Daddy's wearing jeans, sneakers, and a hoodie. Amaya's dad has on a suit, a tie, and shiny brown shoes. Also a frown.

"Jeez, Amaya," he groans. "All this, and you still didn't win?"

Amaya doesn't say anything. What makes it even more shocking is that *I* do.

"She did win," I say.

"What?" Amaya's dad turns to me.

"She did win," I repeat. "All these orders helped our classroom win bragging rights and a trip to Pizza Zone."

"Pizza Zone, huh?" Amaya's dad sighs, then nods at Daddy. "Well, I guess we'll be doing special deliveries till midnight, huh?"

"Looks that way," Daddy says. He sticks out his hand. "Darren Sparks, also known as Zoe's dad."

"Michael Shaw," Amaya's dad says, shaking Daddy's hand. "You think they have some carts or dollies around here?"

"I don't know," says Daddy, grunting as he hoists up a box, "but I won't have to go to the gym later if I do this!"

Amaya's dad chuckles, but he still goes off looking for a cart.

Somehow we cram all the boxes into the Jeep. Daddy studies the paper with all the customer addresses and frowns.

"We'll be delivering till summertime!" he mumbles. I laugh and pat his arm. Only one thing to say.

"Daddy, you're being *dramatic*!"

Epilogue

Four to Six Weeks Later . . .

April 24 is now my favorite day in the universe.

It's the day I *finally* hear, "Zoe Sparks to the main office, please," over the intercom in Mr. Boyd's classroom. It's the day I *finally* see Principal Bledsoe waiting for me with a smile on her face and A PACKAGE IN HER HAND!

"Is that what I think it is?" I ask her, fighting not to jump up and down like a little kid.

"Yes, ma'am," Principal Bledsoe says. "I'm happy to announce that this is an orange Horizon WordPro GT. Know anyone who might want this?"

"Pretty sure I do," I say, taking the box. "Finally! Zoe Sparks is complete!"

Principal Bledsoe laughs and shakes her head.

"All right, Zoe Sparks, back to class," she says.

I don't walk, I don't run. I *float* down the hall to class. The box stays with me the rest of the day.

"You're not gonna open it?" Felix asks me at lunch when I cover the box with napkins before eating my ravioli.

"Nope! Gonna wait till I get home."

"Seriously? You ran your mouth about this thing for months, and you're not instantly ripping it open?"

"Felix, you only get one first time to open a new WordPro."

Felix stops mid-bite and pretends to choke.

"There's something wrong with you."

"There's something wrong with everyone, Fe Fe."

When Daddy picks me up after school, he takes one look at my box and grins.

"Look out, world, Zoe Sparks done got her machine!"

"*Look out* is right," I tell him. "Bestselling stories are gonna come from this thing!"

"So why's it still in the box?" Daddy asks.

"I want to open it at home, in my room," I say. "With Zoe-hype music and maybe a candle, and some sparkling cider."

"Dramatic!" Daddy says in a horrible British accent.

"Passionate!"

Okay, so I don't have the sparkling cider, and Mom won't let me light one of her candles. But Mark comes into my room with his guitar and plays a pretty dope riff while I carefully scissor the box open.

"So that's it, huh," he says when I pull the laptop from the box.

"Yeah," I say.

It is the perfect weight. It is the perfect size. It is the perfect shade of orange.

"I think I have the perfect bag for this," I say, diving under my bed to search for the orange-and-tan messenger bag I got from our trip to California last year. I find shoes, a sweatshirt, and plenty of used tissues (yuck!) before I spot the bag. I open it up and start to slide the WordPro inside when I see something that makes me freeze.

"Ho-ly sh—"

"Hey, hey! Language, Zoe Sparks!" Mark interrupts.

"Shazam; I was gonna say *shazam*!" I tell him. I open the bag wide so he can see inside. "Bet you wanna say the same thing!"

Mark's fingers freeze on his fretboard.

"Wait. Is that . . . ?"

"Yup!" I nod. "Two hundred and thirteen dollars!"

I smack myself on the forehead as it all comes back to me. When Mom told me I shouldn't walk around with so much cash in my pencil case, I stashed what I had in my messenger bag to keep it safe. The bag must've gotten kicked farther and farther under my bed with time, and I completely forgot about the money being in there!

"Well, big bro, I guess *technically* this is yours," I say. "Unless you wanna count me doing all those loads of your dirty laundry as payment."

"Uhhhhh, no, I'll take the cash," Mark says.

"But if I give you the cash, it'll mean I *technically* overpaid you. All those loads of funky underwear and socks. Plus, the CRIM did get that highlight during Young Journalist Week, remember? That's kinda like payment, you know."

"Zoe!"

"Okay, okay!" I say, handing him the money. Mark had been sooo excited to hear that Channel 54 News picked the story I wrote about the CRIM—along with Amaya's story about kids having to split their living time between parents—for Young Journalist Week. My opinion? That alone should've let me off the owing-him hook. The band has booked, like, three gigs since that feature!

"I should come to your room more often!" he laughs.

"Or not."

Everyone's in a good mood by dinner, even when we discover that all Mom made is a salad on steroids. Corn, black beans, shredded cheese, boiled eggs, broccoli, carrots—she basically emptied the whole refrigerator into the salad bowl.

"Is this . . . it?" Daddy's the first to ask.

"Nope; we have rolls," Mom says. I guess that makes it a tiny bit better, especially since they're Hawaiian rolls. "I'm trying something a little different."

"It looks delish!" I say, piling salad on my plate.

"Zoe, really?" Mom asks. "You're gonna eat with that thing?"

I pat my napkin-covered WordPro, which is in my lap.

"Mom, do you know how hard I worked for this?"

"I know how far I drove for that!" Daddy says.

"It'll all be worth it, Daddy," I tell him. "You just wait and see!"

"Oh, I believe you, Zo Zo." Daddy takes a bite of salad and wipes his mouth. "And since we're celebrating the arrival of this wonderful laptop, I might as well share some news of my own."

Daddy pauses dramatically while we all lean forward.

"I was offered a job this morning!"

"What? They offered you the job?" Mom exclaims. "They better! After, what? Three rounds of interviews?"

"Yeah, it was intense," Daddy says. "But worth it."

"That's awesome, Dad," Mark says, his mouth full of ranch dressing–drenched salad. Gross! "Where you working?"

Daddy smiles.

"I'm glad you ask, son," he says. "I'm going to be the food-service manager for Kentwood High School."

Mark chokes on a roll.

"Wait, what?" he says when he recovers. "You're going to serve our lunch?"

"I'm sure I will sometimes," Daddy says. "But I'll also be overseeing the people who do."

"I am *so* glad I'm graduating," Mark says. I laugh. Until I remember one thing.

"Ummm, Daddy?" I say. "No offense, but do you think you could maybe get them to lay you off? In, like, two years maybe?"

"Zoe!" Mom says, with plenty of shock in her voice. "I can't with you."

Daddy, on the other hand, thinks it's hilarious.

"Sorry, Zo Zo, but I plan to be there for a looooong time. Gotta see my baby girl through high school," he says, wiggling his eyebrows. "And somebody's gotta keep an eye on you and Felix."

"Daddy!"

This sooo cannot be happening right now! I cover my face with my hand while everyone else cracks up.

"All right, all right," Daddy says, stopping the torture. He looks at his plate, then at Mom. "Wait a second. Mark gets a restaurant dinner for his Berklee news, and all I get is salad? What's up with that?"

Yikes, he's right! When Mark got his acceptance letter

for Berklee College of Music, we all went to Antonelli's to celebrate, and I even got to order off the adult menu.

"Well, if you had told me!" Mom says, swatting his arm.

"Mm-hmm," Daddy says. "Well, there's only one way to turn this into a *real* celebration."

Daddy stands up and opens the freezer.

"Zo Zo, you thinkin' what I'm thinkin'?"

"Item number 0784!" I call.

For everyone who's not a top seller like me, that's the classic chocolate chip.

Perfect sell.

ACKNOWLEDGMENTS

I have to thank God for keeping this story in my heart for years before I decided to write it. Thank you to my parents for taking my fundraiser order forms to your friends and coworkers; I now understand what that's like! ☺ Thank you to my children—Bianca, Ricky, Micaiah, Natalia, and Zackery—for bringing countless fundraiser packets home and providing me with products that weren't always good and were always way too expensive! ☺ Don't be afraid to work hard for the important prizes in life!

To agent extraordinaire, Hannah, thank you for keeping me calm with all the twists and turns of my 2023 books! A hard labor makes the delivery that much more cherished!

Thank you to the entire Crown team for your careful eyes on this project. Special thanks to Phoebe and Daniela for your support during "The Title Chronicles of Zoe Sparks!"

"Be Better" was my family's theme for 2022. It's a phrase I often heard Kobe Bryant say, so naturally, I tattooed it on my writing arm and drilled it into the minds of my children. Each day, strive to be better than you were the day before, even if only by a fraction. That's progress. To my young readers with big dreams, prepare to be amazed at what happens when you get ready . . . get set . . . GO!!!

Favorites with Kelly J. Baptist

What is your favorite color?
Turquoise

Who is your favorite athlete?
Kobe Bryant

What is your favorite food?
Soul food

Who is your favorite poet?
Elizabeth Acevedo

What was your favorite middle-grade book when you were a child?
Everything by Mildred D. Taylor!

ABOUT THE AUTHOR

Kelly J. Baptist is the inaugural winner of the We Need Diverse Books short-story contest. Her story is featured in the WNDB anthology *Flying Lessons & Other Stories* and inspired her first full-length novel, *Isaiah Dunn Is My Hero,* which received starred reviews from *Booklist* and *Publishers Weekly,* and which the *New York Times* praised as "inventive and heartfelt," and its sequel, *Isaiah Dunn Saves the Day.* Her middle-grade novel *The Swag Is in the Socks* received starred reviews from *The Bulletin* and *Booklist,* which called it "an excellent read-alike to Jacqueline Woodson's *Harbor Me* or Janae Marks' *From the Desk of Zoe Washington.*" Kelly is also the author of the picture book *The Electric Slide and Kai* and the middle-grade novel in verse *Eb & Flow.* She wrote *Ready, Set, Dough!* as an exploration of a critical question: Does anyone ever win the top prize in these never-ending school fundraisers? Kelly lives in southwest Michigan with her five amazing children.

kellyiswrite.com

READ MORE BOOKS BY
KELLY J. BAPTIST!

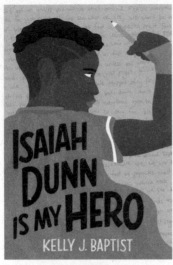

A *Booklist* Best Book
of the Year

"Isaiah's voice rings true."
—*Kirkus Reviews*

Midland Authors Children's
Fiction Award Winner

"Hand to fans of Jason Reynolds
and Jacqueline Woodson."
—*Booklist*